Captured in Colombia

Jeanette Windle

ACE *Publications*

Captured in Colombia
by Jeanette Windle

Cover illustration by Marie Tabler
Copy Editor: Julia C. Hansen
Book design by Amy Haynes
Proofreaders: Sheri Harshaw and Sally Bradley

Copyright © 1999 by Jeanette Windle

Published by
PACE *Publications*
PO Box 1982
Independence, MO 64055

Formerly published in a trilogy form as
Adventures in South America
by Multnomah Youth, Sisters, Oregon
(Now out of print)

Printed in the United States of America
Set in Times New Roman 12 point
ISBN 0-918407-16-8

Captured in Colombia

by Jeanette Windle

Watch for future books in this series!

**Parker Twins books by
Jeanette Windle**

**Cave of the Inca Rey
Jungle Hideout
Captured in Colombia**

Contents

Prologue

A Deadly Flood

It was the stillness and grayness that caught Justin's attention. He stopped struggling against the tightly knotted ropes cutting into his wrists long enough to draw a hot breath into burning lungs. The cliff-top above them was empty. The hoarse voices and the jingle of mules' harnesses had long since died away. The hail of pebbles and grit that had stung his face was over now, too.

No birds twittered in the wind-stunted tamaracks. And not a single cricket scraped the incessant song Justin had heard since his captors dragged him into the guerrilla camp. His sister and uncle, working at their own bonds, were silent. They had said all there was to say. Even the tangled branches of the bent cypress and junipers that lined the narrow creek and grew up the steep sides of the canyon hung silent and still. The only sound was a faint rushing in the distance that carried the promise of a faraway waterfall.

An onlooker might have thought it was snow that cast a cloak of ghostly white across the ground, the camp, and the three people tied fast to a branch that overhung the river . . . if it weren't for the strange breathlessness and the taste of sulfur in the air. Even the prints of men and animals, and the dead grass where tents had stood just a short time ago, were slowly being covered.

Justin blew uselessly at the cloud of grayish-white that drifted down from the evergreen needles to blind his eyes and choke his nostrils. Sweat trickled into his eyes and traced dark streaks down his face. He no longer felt the early morning chill of this high Andes gully.

Most of Justin's attention was focused on a broken piece of glass on the ground that offered hope of escape. But a corner of his mind eventually became aware that the quiet of the imagined distant waterfall had been transformed until it now resembled the grinding of an enormous cement mixer, churning rock and concrete in its massive metal belly. He looked up in surprise—then froze in fear.

Far up the mountain canyon, the eruption had fulfilled its promise. Released by the volcanic heat of the simmering Andes peak, thousands of tons of melted snow had plummeted downward, gobbling up dirt, boulders, trees, and any animals unfortunate enough to step in its path. Squeezed to unbelievable heights by the narrow canyon walls, the churning gray-brown mud flow—or *lahar*—now swept down the gully with enough force to bury a town.

The distant wall of mud and ice that met Justin's stunned gaze seemed to crawl at a turtle's pace, but Justin saw it scrape tangled trees and bushes from the canyon walls with the ease of a toddler snapping a toothpick in two. He saw a leaping wave sweep a boulder the size of a small house from the clifftop. It bobbed a moment, then disappeared below the surface.

Justin now pulled frantically at the ropes that held his

hands outstretched overhead. Warmth trickled down his arms as the harsh strands cut into his wrists. He glanced upstream once more. Already the solid, gray-brown mass had doubled in size as it moved closer. He could see uprooted trees tossing about on the crest of the wave.

He tugged again, desperately, at his bonds, but there was no more time. Towering above the three small figures on the canyon floor, the *lahar* was now swallowing, one by one, the long line of evergreens that shaded the creek only half-a-mile upstream.

Justin stopped struggling. No longer afraid, he stared in helpless horror as the wave of mud and ice swept down upon the camp.

Chapter 1

A Steaming Peak

"Justin, are we riding clear to Colombia like this?"

Nose pressed to the small round window of the DC-3, Justin Parker watched the distant carpet of the jungle canopy sweep under the wing just below him. A heavy wind tossed the treetops into a choppy, dusty-green sea.

"Justin!" his twin sister, Jenny, repeated above the roar of the propellers. Running his fingers impatiently through short, red curls, the lean thirteen-year-old reluctantly looked away from a mass of darkening clouds that drifted across the horizon.

Justin grinned as he noticed his sister's pale face and the folded paper bag in her hands, but he quickly changed his freckled face to a look of concern as he exclaimed, "Jenny, you look awful!"

"Thanks a lot!" Jenny answered, gold-brown eyes flashing indignantly. She sat up straight. One slim, tanned hand used the paper bag as a fan while the other pushed back damp, dark curls. But as another wind gust shook the plane, Jenny slumped back in the hard seat and moaned, "I'm going to be sick!"

"It's the altitude," Justin explained patiently. "These old planes don't have pressurized cabins."

Justin and Jenny Parker were opposites in more than just appearance. Tall for his age, Justin was usually calm and even-tempered, but those who knew him well understood a certain stubborn set of his jaw. Steady, blue-green eyes noticed everything that went on around him.

As tall as her brother, Jenny moved through life at a run. But a strong streak of common sense rounded out her outgoing personality.

A flight attendant, her dark hair tucked up inside a blue cap, smiled at the twins and held out a tray. Jenny shook her head violently, but Justin reached for a plastic cup half-filled with Coca-Cola®.

He had barely lifted the cup to his mouth when his seat seemed to drop away beneath him. Justin grabbed for his armrest as his stomach leapt into his throat. When the plane leveled off, he looked at the almost-empty cup in his hand, then at the ceiling as something wet dripped down his neck. Another drop of Coca-Cola® landed on his freckled nose.

"*Disculpa*! I am so sorry!" said the flight attendant, wiping a handful of paper towels across the light panel above Justin. Glancing around, Justin saw that he wasn't the only one to lose his drink.

"The plane fell!" Jenny gasped. "Uncle Pete, what happened!"

Across the aisle, a tall man with the build of a youthful Santa Claus wiped a paper towel across a full beard as red as Justin's hair. "We hit a down draft. The plane just dropped a few meters—nothing to worry about."

"Nothing to worry about!" Jenny wailed, clutching her paper bag again.

Shaking his head at the remainder of his drink, Justin handed the cup to the flight attendant. "I guess I didn't want it, anyway!"

"Oh, no!" Jenny wailed. Justin swung around as she motioned toward the window. The bank of storm clouds he had seen earlier was now just ahead—a menacing, dark mountain looming over the small plane. Moments later the interior of the plane turned to night as the storm closed around them.

The twins clutched their armrests as the small plane shook violently. Rain streamed down the windows. Looking over Justin's shoulder, Jenny gasped, "Justin, look! The wings!"

Justin again pressed his nose to the window. Just outside the window, the propeller fought against the driving rain. Lightning lit up the misty interior of the cloud, and Justin swallowed hard as he watched the wings shiver under another blast of wind.

As another flash of lightning crashed just beyond the wing tip, a light went on across the aisle. Swaying gently with the movements of the plane, Uncle Pete calmly held a sheaf of papers up to the dim glow of the cabin light. The man seated next to him, his eyes squeezed shut, was muttering what Justin guessed to be Spanish prayers.

Jenny eyed her uncle indignantly. "Uncle Pete, how can you work in this? We could be killed!"

Uncle Pete raised reddish-brown eyebrows at the anxious expressions of his niece and nephew. "You aren't worried, are you, kids? These planes are used to this kind of weather. They don't have the power to get up above the clouds."

Laying the sheaf of papers carefully on his lap, he added thoughtfully, "Of course, this particular plane is a World War

II leftover. I don't suppose it's been maintained too well . . . "

As the sound of an infuriated kitten exploded from Jenny, he added hastily, "There's nothing to worry about, kids! Look. We're already breaking through the storm. We'll be in Santa Cruz in twenty minutes."

"And, no," he answered Jenny's original question as he turned back to his paperwork, "we won't be flying this crate clear to Colombia. We'll be flying to Bogota tomorrow in a Boeing 727." Glancing at Jenny's still-pale face, he added, "With a pressurized, air-conditioned cabin, and well above any kind of weather!"

A top consultant for a major oil company, Triton Oil, Pete Parker spent much of his time jetting around the world, taking care of any problems that arose at the company's scattered work bases. His special hobby was befriending missionaries in the many countries he visited on business, and he liked to blame his size on their hospitality and the many new dishes he had to sample.

Justin and Jenny Parker had always looked forward to the interesting gifts and stories Uncle Pete brought on visits to their Seattle home. When Uncle Pete decided to combine some vacation time with business in the small South American country of Bolivia, he had invited his nephew and niece to come along.

Exploring Inca ruins less than two weeks ago, on a visit to the highland capital of La Paz, the twins had encountered a pair of artifact smugglers. Their escape from the cursed Cave of the Inca Rey had shown their young guide, Pedro, a descendant of the ancient Incas, both the love and power of God.

Just this past week, at one of Triton Oil's jungle bases, they had helped bring about the destruction of a cocaine lab and the arrest of a ring of drug dealers. Then, just this morning, as they boarded the DC-3 to leave the Bolivian jungle behind, Uncle Pete had received a request to check out the company's main Latin American office in Bogota, the capital city of Colombia.

〰〰   〰〰   〰〰

It was noon the next day when the loudspeaker at the front of the Boeing 727 first-class cabin announced that they were now over Colombian airspace and would be landing in Bogota within the hour. Their appetites by now restored, Justin and Jenny bent over the lunch the airline had provided.

Justin lifted the foil that covered his plate and sniffed gratefully at the perfect sirloin steak that nestled beside a baked potato. Adjusting the flow of cool air above her, Jenny sighed with contentment as she peeled the gold foil from a wedge of French cheese.

The flight attendant had just cleared away the trays when the warning light above their seats blinked on. The twins quickly fastened their seat belts for the landing. Jenny now sat beside the window, but Justin bent his neck to look over her shoulder. Still far below, a circle of snow-capped peaks enclosed a vast valley. As the plane curved downward, Justin could make out a patchwork of dark-green evergreens and yellow-green mountain meadows.

"Uncle Pete, isn't Colombia on the equator?" he asked with surprise. "I thought it would be all jungle."

"Yes, it is on the equator," Uncle Pete answered without lifting his eyes from his spread-out briefcase contents. "And there is plenty of jungle. But the Andes Mountains here form a valley at about 8500 feet in elevation. It's cool enough to have vegetation much like the mountains back home."

"It's beautiful!" Jenny said with awe, as pine forests and meadows bright with wildflowers rolled away below.

"Why are the capital cities all so high?" Justin asked, remembering the vast mountain crater in which the Bolivian capital of La Paz sat.

"Most of the main cities in the Andes were built in high mountain valleys," Uncle Pete answered, absently shuffling through a stack of computer readouts, "to get away from the heat and danger of the jungles. The Andes here in Colombia get a lot more rain, so they have more vegetation—"

His explanation was interrupted by an excited squeal from Jenny. "Hey, look at that! That mountain is smoking!"

Justin leaned over to study the mountain peak his sister was pointing to. The slightly lopsided peak was as snowcovered as its neighbors. But sure enough, from the snow fields rose clouds of steam—as though the mountain were indeed smoking.

"Is that a volcano?" he asked curiously.

"Most of the Andean mountains were once active volcanoes," Uncle Pete said, looking up again. "Hmm, that one does look like it's still alive! It must be the Nevada del Ruiz."

Laying down his papers, he added thoughtfully, "That peak made world news not too long ago."

Jenny could always sense a story. "Please tell us about it, Uncle Pete!"

Uncle Pete closed his briefcase and sat back. "Well, like most of its neighbors, the Nevada del Ruiz had been asleep—dormant—for many years. Then one day it woke up and blew its top. It wasn't much of a blow as volcanoes go—not much lava flow at all. But the heat of the volcano melted much of its snow and ice cap. Half the mountainside washed down, creating a mud flow more than forty feet deep that wiped out thousands of farms. One entire town of twenty-thousand people remains buried under the mud."

Justin eyed the steaming peak respectfully as the plane banked and left the mountain range behind. Still far below sprawled the city of Bogota. Box-like skyscrapers reached for a cloudless sky, and a maze of roads climbed over and under each other like some toy construction set.

"It's so big!" Jenny gasped.

"More than eight million people," Uncle Pete commented. "Bigger than New York City."

"Well, there should be some good shopping in a place that size!" Jenny concluded with satisfaction.

The landing wheels touched down just minutes later. Slinging his hand luggage over his shoulder, Justin pulled his jacket tight against a brisk wind that whistled through the cracks of the inflated plastic tube that connected the Boeing 727 to the airport terminal.

As they trudged up the long corridor from the unloading gate, the twins eyed with interest the shops that lined both sides. They had stopped to admire some hand-blown glass swans when a voice questioned softly, *"Café, señores?"*

The two children whirled around. A square booth stood in the center of the wide hallway. On its side the words *"Asociación de Cafeteros Colombianos"* were written under a picture of a man dressed in a poncho and sombrero. On the counter, a tall percolator steamed next to a collection of fine china cups. A smiling, dark-haired girl leaned over the counter. Catching their puzzled expressions, she repeated in careful English, "Would you like to try a cup of Colombian coffee?"

Jenny grimaced. "No, thanks! I don't like coffee."

Uncle Pete reached over their heads to accept a cup of coffee. "Try it, kids! You've never tasted coffee like this."

Justin breathed in the rich smell of the percolator. "I guess I'll try a cup!"

"I will make you my specialty," the girl offered. " *'Café con leche'*—coffee with milk."

Justin raised reddish-brown eyebrows in surprise as he took a cautious sip of the milky-brown liquid. It was sweet and strong but had none of the bitter taste he usually associated with coffee.

Jenny doubtfully sipped her own cup, then her eyes lit up. "Mmmm! It tastes almost like hot chocolate!"

The hostess smiled with pleasure. "It is pure, mountain-grown Colombian coffee—the best in the world!"

Jenny giggled. "Just like the commercials back home!"

Uncle Pete set down his cup. "OK, kids, we need to check through customs and pick up our baggage."

In the center of the long corridor ahead stood what looked like a metal doorway just wide enough for one person. At table height beside it, a conveyor belt carried hand luggage through a similar—though much smaller—door. Soldiers in camouflage, machine guns cradled across muscled bare arms, made sure that every passenger passed through the doorway.

The passenger in front of the Parkers had just set his handbag on the conveyor belt when someone with an American accent called, "Mr. Parker?"

A young man of medium height with clipped, dark hair pushed unhindered past the armed guards and stepped around the metal door. His gray business suit didn't hide the tough, wide-shouldered build of an athlete. *Or a soldier,* as Justin thought.

His dark-brown eyes were unsmiling as he handed a card to Uncle Pete. "Pete Parker, Triton Oil, right? I'm Steve Cardoza, American embassy. I'm here to pick you up."

"Well, I appreciate this," Uncle Pete answered, studying the card with a puzzled expression. "But it isn't necessary.

I'm expecting one of my own men to pick me up."

"I'm afraid that won't be possible," Steve Cardoza answered shortly. He glanced around at the still-waiting passengers. "I'll explain later. This place is too public. Right now, let's get your things cleared through customs."

An impatient official was now waiting for the Parkers to move ahead. As Uncle Pete stepped through the metal doorway, Mr. Cardoza swung Jenny's handbag to the conveyor belt. Jenny hung back. "Why do we have to go through that? What is it?"

"It's an X-ray machine," Mr. Cardoza explained shortly. "It makes sure you're not bringing in anything you aren't supposed to."

"Drugs, you mean," Justin commented, remembering the customs search in Bolivia.

The dark-haired embassy aide looked grim. "Not drugs. Bombs!"

The surprised children meekly stepped single-file through the doorway. As Justin walked through, an alarm sounded and a red light above the doorway began blinking. An unsmiling soldier moved to cut him off, then stepped back as Justin sheepishly pulled out the pocket flashlight that had triggered the alarm.

Justin noticed many other heavily armed soldiers as they pulled their suitcases from the baggage conveyor and went through another customs check. When they had repacked their suitcases, Steve Cardoza flagged a porter who wheeled the luggage to the parking zone. Here, too, alert and unsmiling soldiers patrolled back and forth, machine guns held ready across their chests.

"Wow! Is there a war going on?" Justin whispered to Jenny as Mr. Cardoza unlocked the back of a dark-blue Toyota

Vanette and tossed in the suitcases.

Giving the minivan a disappointed look, Jenny whispered back, "That's an embassy car? I figured it would be red, white, and blue with an American flag flying from the top!"

The embassy aide obviously had sharp ears. As he motioned them into the minivan, he remarked grimly, "In Colombia we'd rather not stand out! And yes, you could say there's a war going on!"

Mr. Cardoza expertly maneuvered the minivan through a long line of buses and taxis. Justin was surprised to pass several more terminal buildings, the signs in front announcing the services of dozens of airlines. AVIANCA, the national Colombian airline, predominated. One of the terminals was air force, Justin guessed, eyeing the fighters and combat helicopters outside.

Mr. Cardoza turned onto a broad boulevard. Squat, gray factories stretched out alongside towering office buildings.

"Just like Seattle," Justin commented, feeling suddenly homesick for the busy streets of his home city. Then, as the embassy aide suddenly slammed on the brakes and cut across a lane of traffic, he added dryly, "Well, maybe not quite!"

Justin counted five lanes clearly marked on the road flowing toward the city, but he was startled to notice that seven or eight vehicles rushed abreast ahead of the van. With total disregard for traffic rules, the smaller cars zipped back and forth across the path of busses and trucks while the larger vehicles seemed ready to ram anything that got in their way.

Jenny squealed as Mr. Cardoza changed lanes again, almost under the wheels of a massive refrigerated truck. Glancing back, the embassy aide's bronzed face broke into a grin. "It's not much like driving back home, but it's really a lot of fun when you get used to it. Kind of like the Indy 500."

Justin suddenly sat up straight. Just ahead, a mass of blackened rubble and the shattered remnants of a tall building broke the solid line of factories. "Wow! What happened there?" he asked. "It looks like the place exploded!"

Over the back of the seat, Justin could see their driver's strong hands tighten on the steering wheel. "Yesterday's bomb," he answered grimly. "The reason for all the stepped-up security at the airport."

"You mentioned a war, Mr. Cardoza," Uncle Pete spoke up quietly. "I haven't had much access to the news in the last couple of weeks, but I understood that the guerrillas here in Colombia were in the middle of peace talks with the government. I wouldn't have brought the kids otherwise."

"Gorillas!" Jenny exclaimed, looking puzzled. "How can monkeys talk to a government?"

Uncle Pete's sudden cough sounded suspiciously like a laugh, but he explained patiently, "Not the kind of gorillas you find in a zoo. *Guerrillas* are bands of terrorists who want to overthrow the government so they can take over the country for themselves. Is that essentially right, Mr. Cardoza?"

"Just call me Steve," the dark-haired embassy aide said absently. Then he added, "You're exactly right, Mr. Parker. And yes, the guerrillas have consented to peace talks with the government. But as you can see, there are plenty of stray bands still tossing bombs."

"Well, I appreciate your concern for the safety of American citizens," Uncle Pete commented. "But I still don't understand. There must be dozens of Americans flying in and out of Bogota every day. Surely the embassy doesn't go to the trouble of picking them all up every time there has been a bombing!"

He added quietly, "There's obviously something else going on here. Maybe it's time you told me where you are taking us—and why my own men didn't come to pick me up."

"You'll see where we're going in just a minute," Steve answered politely. "My boss will be there to meet you. I'd rather let him explain."

They were now driving through a quiet residential neighborhood. Just then they turned into a narrow side street lined with four-story brick buildings. High-pitched, excited voices broke the quiet. Steve slammed on the brakes as a group of dark-haired children kicked a tattered soccer ball right under the wheels of the minivan.

A shrill bark caught Justin's attention. Pressing his nose to the window, he realized that what looked like a dirty-white dust mop on the sidewalk was actually a small dog. The dog rolled over and whined with contentment as a girl—long, dark hair covering her face—leaned down to scratch its belly.

The children scattered as Steve leaned on the horn. Muttering under his breath, he pulled up in front of one of the townhouses. Only a pair of soldiers with tiny American flags on the shoulders of their uniforms gave any indication that the building was anything other than an ordinary house.

"This is the American embassy guest house," Steve informed them as they piled out of the minivan. Nodding at the soldiers' salute, he took out a bunch of keys. The twins watched in awe as he unlocked first one, then another of a series of five locks. "We had a hand grenade tossed in here a couple of months ago. So we're careful about who enters embassy property."

Picking up his suitcase as Steve swung open the heavy metal door, Justin glanced down the long street. The children were still playing, the small, dusty-white dog frisking around their feet. Suddenly, Justin heard a shrill whistle, and the dog broke free from the group of children. Just as Justin stepped into a wide, tiled hall, the dog dashed between his legs and into the hall.

"Get that dog!" Steve slammed the door shut and leaped for the dog. As he skidded across the polished tiles, the dog dashed back toward the door. Dropping his suitcase, Justin lunged for the dog.

Rolling over, Justin sat up, clutching the bundle of fur tightly. Noticing a grimy handkerchief tied around a front foreleg, he stroked the trembling animal gently. "Did you hurt yourself?"

He untied the dirty cloth, and a rolled-up piece of paper fell to the ground. Unrolling the paper, Justin stared with astonishment as he recognized the insignia that had been cut from some brochure and pasted to one end of the sheet of cheap notebook paper. It was the insignia of Triton Oil.

"Well, what is it?" Jenny asked impatiently, peering over his shoulder. Then Uncle Pete reached down and lifted the piece of paper from Justin's hands. The hall fell silent as he read aloud, "Release our men at once, or suffer grave consequences."

Chapter 2

Trouble for Triton Oil

"Give me the dog!" Justin blinked in astonishment as Steve snatched the dog away. Carrying him across the hall, he ran his hands over the animal, even checking its mouth. "No explosives!" he pronounced at last with relief.

Seeing the twins' look of surprise, he explained, "I've seen bombs delivered in some pretty strange ways."

As Steve put down the dog, Justin suddenly thought of something. Swinging open the heavy door, he peered down the street. It was now empty.

"Hey! Shut that door!" Something furry brushed against Justin's legs. Before he could move, the dusty-white dog had dashed around the corner of the building. Steve clapped Justin on the shoulder as he started to apologize. "Don't worry about it, kid. The dog probably wouldn't have helped us anyway."

He too studied the empty street. "That was good thinking, though. I'd say someone paid those kids to deliver this message."

As they stepped back inside, a tall, thin man with honey-colored skin and tight black curls came down a wide staircase at the end of the hall. "What's all the commotion, Steve?"

He held out his hand to Uncle Pete as Steve introduced him. "This is Martin Bascom, Secretary to the American ambassador here in Bogota—and my boss! Mr. Bascom, Pete Parker, consultant for Triton Oil."

Mr. Bascom led the group into a large living room off the hall while Steve explained what had happened. As they all sat down, Uncle Pete handed the diplomat the slip of paper they had found on the dog. "This seems to be directed at my company. What, exactly, is going on here?"

Instead of answering Uncle Pete's question, Mr. Bascom asked, "Mr. Parker, how much do you know about the situation here in Colombia?"

Uncle Pete rubbed his beard thoughtfully. "Well, I know that Colombia has one of the best records of democratic government in South America. They are not a wealthy country, but they've made a lot of social and economic advances over the last thirty years—including the development of their oil industry."

He added, "I also know that in the last few years guerrillas have brought the country to the brink of civil war and threatened to destroy every advance the government has made."

Mr. Bascom looked satisfied. "That's right! Guerrilla bands are the plague of Colombia. Each group is determined to overthrow the elected government and put themselves into power. The biggest is FARC—which is the Spanish abbreviation for the 'Armed Revolutionary Forces of Colombia.' Then there is the ELN—or the National Liberation Army. And of course, there are dozens of smaller groups. Many are being funded by the drug trade."

As the twins sat up with sudden interest, he added, "Drug traffickers use guerrillas as their private armies—paying them in weapons. Many of these guerrilla bands are better armed than the Colombian army. And they will do just about anything to achieve their goals—from tossing a bomb that kills dozens of innocent bystanders to blowing up the pipelines that carry oil across the country."

Uncle Pete's hazel eyes sharpened with interest. "Is that where Triton Oil comes in?"

Mr. Bascom nodded. "At the moment the major guerrilla groups have signed a cease-fire with the government. But there are still plenty of smaller groups running around loose. Two days ago, one of your American engineers was checking out your base in the eastern plains when he discovered two men setting an explosive to the pipeline near the oil camp. With the help of some local oil workers, he managed to capture them and turn them over to the Colombian police.

"It turns out that the two men were both members of some small guerrilla band. The Triton Oil office here has already received a phone call this morning, threatening to take action against the company if their men are not released."

An expression of worry clouded the man's face, but Mr. Bascom said firmly, "We really don't think there is much danger, but as a precaution, we have temporarily shut down your office and placed security guards at the homes of the two Americans who work there. Your head of operations here in Bogota asked if we would have you picked up at the airport."

"I certainly appreciate your cooperation," Uncle Pete said, glancing at his watch, "but I would like to meet with the head of operations as soon as possible. Can that be arranged?"

"Of course!" Mr. Bascom stood up. "I'll give him a call and take you over myself."

The twins jumped up eagerly, and Uncle Pete frowned. "A business meeting is no place for you kids. You'd better stay here, where it's safe."

Catching their look of disappointment, Mr. Bascom raised a hand. "There's no need of that. Lieutenant Steve Cardoza is on loan from the U.S. Marine Corps to help with our security. He will be responsible for your safety while you are here. The children will be perfectly safe doing some sightseeing with him."

Justin eyed with satisfaction the muscles that pressed against the seams of Steve's civilian clothes. "I *knew* you were a soldier!"

With a grin, the broad-shouldered Marine saluted smartly, then motioned toward the door. "Let's go, kids!"

〰   〰   〰

The quiet streets surrounding the embassy guest house could have been any middle-class neighborhood in North America. As Steve drove back onto a major thoroughfare, he asked, "Well, kids, what would you like to see first?"

"A pamphlet we got on the plane said something about the Gold Museum," Justin said.

"I want to go shopping," argued Jenny. "We saw the open-air market in Bolivia. It was pretty exciting, with all the Indian ladies sitting on the ground, selling their fruits and vegetables."

Steve looked from one to the other. "Tell you what! I'll show you how we do our shopping here in Bogota. Then we'll hit that museum you mentioned."

Moments later, the minivan turned into a large parking lot. Across the front of a two-story glass and brick building several blocks long, a massive sign announced, "UNICENTRO."

"Hey, this is just a mall!" Jenny exclaimed with disappointment as Steve herded them toward the main entrance.

Inside, Justin read the signs that lined the vast, tiled corridor. "Wendy's, Burger King, Sears—just like back home!"

Steve grinned. "I'm afraid shopping in Bogota isn't much different than in the U.S."

Jenny was inspecting a dress displayed in the window of an exclusive boutique. "Except for the prices! Look at this . . . $2,249! Who can afford to shop here?"

Leaving the mall with their savings intact, they drove toward the center of the city. Modern skyscrapers elbowed white colonial buildings with fancy iron balconies and red tile roofs. Studying a space-age office building whose tilted roof jutted toward the sky like a fighter jet taking off, Justin commented, "I sure didn't expect everything to be so modern and beautiful."

"Yeah, I don't understand why anyone would want to overthrow the government when they have such a nice country," Jenny agreed. "Those guerrillas must be awful people!"

"You kids have only seen the best part of the city!" Steve commented, turning the minivan onto a narrow avenue lined with old, gray factory buildings. Soon the factories gave way to grime-stained apartment buildings. Doors swung on broken hinges, and scraps of lumber and cardboard darkened smashed windows. Startled, the two children sat up straight as even these buildings were left behind.

The houses just ahead—if such they could be called— clung to the edges of a vast garbage dump. Scavenged boards, tin, and even old tires were nailed together to form crude shelters. Lines of threadbare laundry dangled between low roofs pieced together from scraps of metal.

"Hey, look at that!" exclaimed Jenny.

Under the flat bed of an abandoned trailer was a cardboard box that had once protected a freezer. An entrance had been cut in the front, and a sheet of torn plastic stretched over the top to keep out the rain. But what caught the twins' attention was the small boy whose tangle-haired, dark head was pillowed on a gunny sack in the makeshift doorway. A ragged man's sweater was his only protection against the chill mountain winds.

"Does he *live* there?" Jenny asked in horror. "Where are his parents?"

The grim look was back on Steve's face. "He probably has no parents. There are hundreds of thousands of kids like him on the streets of Colombia. They are called the *gamines*—street urchins. They stay alive by running errands, stealing, even eating garbage.

"You asked about the guerrillas," he added as they left the dump behind. "Many of the guerrillas come from poor families such as these. They've seen their families suffer while most of the country's wealth is concentrated in the hands of just a few."

"No wonder they get mad!" Justin said soberly, looking back at the flimsy cardboard home. "But if the government doesn't want the guerrillas to fight, why don't they do something to help?"

"The government is trying to do something," Steve answered seriously as he turned back onto a major boulevard. "But Colombia isn't a rich country, and improvement is slow. The guerrillas aren't willing to wait. They don't consider themselves criminals. They think of themselves as freedom fighters—fighting to free the poor from what they consider the 'oppression of the rich ruling class.'

"Unfortunately, while some guerrillas are real idealists who want to make the country better for the ordinary people, many just want to grab power and money for themselves. Instead of trying to change their country peacefully, they throw bombs and murder a lot of innocent people."

Glancing at their gloomy faces, he suddenly smiled. "Hey, kids, cheer up! On the whole, Colombia is a beautiful country, and we want you to enjoy your stay here."

Moments later Steve pulled up beside a wide plaza where thick-trunked trees spread leafy branches over stone benches, and marble fountains splashed rainbows in the late afternoon sun. "Come on, kids! You're about to see the most fabulous gold collection in the world."

Steve led the twins through the center of the plaza to a new-looking brick and glass skyscraper. Justin stopped counting stories after the first two dozen and studied the sign above wide glass doors. "Hey, this is a bank! I thought we were going to the Gold Museum!"

Steve grinned. "Yes, it *is*—and we *are!* The Gold Museum is housed in the bank because it contains most of Colombia's national gold reserve."

"You mean it's just a bunch of gold bars?" Jenny asked in disappointment. "Like the American national gold reserve at Fort Knox?"

"You'll have to wait and see," Steve answered. He motioned them into the bank lobby and bought their tickets. When a small group of other tourists had gathered, a guide motioned them toward a broad staircase. An armed Colombian soldier stepped in front of the group, while another brought up the rear.

The guide paused outside a heavy metal door like that of

a bank vault. An armed guard stood in front of the door. As the door swung open, the guide motioned for the group to step forward, one at a time.

"What is he doing?" Jenny asked Steve.

"That door works like the X-ray machine you stepped through at the airport," Steve explained. "They're checking for burglary tools, as well as weapons."

The twins were surprised when Steve reached inside his jacket and pulled out a small pistol. With a rapid stream of Spanish, he handed the pistol and some identification papers to the guard.

"Hey, you sure speak good Spanish!" Justin complemented as the guard handed back Steve's identification and pocketed the pistol.

Steve grinned. "You pick up plenty of Spanish growing up in Southern California. That's what got me transferred to Colombia."

Justin and Jenny followed him into a large, empty room with no windows. Justin noticed a tiny video camera watching them from one corner. Across the room was another vault door. When the entire group was inside, the first door closed behind them.

"They sure aren't taking any chances with their gold, are they?" Jenny giggled a bit nervously as the light dimmed around them.

But her giggles ended in amazed silence as the second door slid open and the crowd of people moved into the lighted vault beyond. A soft yellow glittered on all sides, but not from stacks of heavy gold bars. Behind thick glass display windows, gold bracelets, rings, and necklaces were piled in careless abandon. Odd geometric designs etched cups and plates of solid gold, hammered out centuries before for an Indian noble's table.

"All that remains of Colombia's pre-Spanish riches," Steve said, looking amused at their open-mouthed awe. "It's the largest collection of gold artifacts in the world."

Jenny paused to examine a headdress that gleamed green against the delicate gold-work. Steve looked over her shoulder. "Those stones are emeralds," he told her. "The best coffee in the world isn't all Colombia produces. They also export most of the world's emeralds."

He leaned against a pillar. "You kids go on and look around. I've seen this often enough."

The twins moved slowly along the rows of display windows. They stopped suddenly as a dark-skinned warrior glared firecely at them from behind a mask of solid gold. His outthrust spear guarded a staircase that led to a lower level.

"He isn't real!" Justin said a little shakily as he realized the warrior was carved of some dark wood. From a lifeless chin jutted a pointed, golden beard. The gold helmet on the wooden head was topped with an ornate headdress of red, black, and gold feathers, and emeralds crossed a hammered breastplate. Golden earrings, curled like wood shavings, dangled from deaf ears.

"I knew he wasn't real!" Jenny answered scornfully as she started down the staircase. Justin looked unconvinced, but followed her to the lower level. Here tourists crowded around more showcases, exclaiming expressions of awe and greed in many languages.

Glancing up from an elegantly jeweled crown, Justin suddenly noticed that one face nearby didn't reflect awe or delight at the beauty that filled the vault. Her slim shoulders tight with concentration, a girl about the age of Justin and Jenny pressed against a glass window. The arrow-straight hair that cascaded below her waist was so black that it gleamed blue in the soft light of the display.

The girl moved slightly, and Justin caught a glimpse of delicate, pale features tight with anger. A thin hand hanging at her side clenched and unclenched as she stared at the heaped-up gold. *She must have come in at the last minute or I would have noticed her,* Justin thought. *She isn't like anyone I've ever seen!*

Reading his thoughts with the closeness of long practice, Jenny whispered, "She looks like a princess!"

Eyeing the neat but threadbare clothes, she added, "A princess in disguise, that is!"

"I wonder who she is?" Justin whispered back.

As though she had heard, the girl turned, ice-blue eyes, fringed with impossibly long, black eyelashes, and gave them a disdainful look. Then she turned her back to them.

"Come on, Jenny!" Justin said, flushing with embarrassment as he motioned Jenny toward a large, square glass case that stood alone in the center of the room.

"Wow! Look at that!" They forgot the strange girl as they bent over the lone object displayed in the glass case. Somehow afloat on a tiny artificial lake was a raft of gold logs only six inches long. At one end knelt a paddler, steering the raft with a long golden pole. In the center, his jeweled eyes blindly watching the horizon, stood an Indian prince, his tiny gold adornments hinting his relationship to the warrior upstairs. The haughty lift of the royal chin brought back to Justin's mind the proud face of the girl they had just seen.

"That piece alone could keep every homeless child in Bogota off the streets for a month!" a voice said coldly in the precise, accentless English of a well-educated foreigner. The twins whirled around. Her silky-fine hair falling in a shimmering curtain across her face, the girl they had noticed earlier leaned over the glass case.

"This gold should belong to the people of this country— all of it!" Her eyes were now hot blue sparks as she threw out a slim arm to include the rest of the room. "It should be sold— used to help the poor of this country. Instead, it's kept locked up for a bunch of fat, wealthy tourists to stare at!"

Startled at the bitterness in the girl's voice, Justin answered reasonably, "I thought it *did* belong to the people of Colombia. I mean, they said it was the *national* gold reserve. Doesn't that mean these things belong to everyone?"

"And they are so beautiful!" Jenny broke in, brushing her fingertips over the glass case as though to touch what lay within. She added, "And here, everyone can enjoy them— including the people of Colombia."

"Beauty can't fill a starving stomach!" the other girl answered coldly.

The murmur of tourists filing by filled an awkward silence. Then Jenny turned away. "Come on, Justin! I'm ready to go!"

"Wait! Please! Don't go!" Her voice half-angry, half-pleading, the girl took a step toward them. "I'm . . . " The apology seemed to catch in her throat, then she said, "My name is Estrella."

She pronounced the name Es-stray-ya. As Justin mentally sounded out the strange syllables, she added, "It means 'star' in your language."

Seeing Jenny's unfriendly expression, Justin held out his hand. "Why don't we start over. My name is Justin Parker, and this is my sister, Jenny. We're visiting your country with my Uncle Pete. He's an oil consultant. You may have seen the signs for Triton Oil. That's his company."

The girl's long lashes dropped to conceal a sudden gleam of satisfaction as Justin hurried on, "You sure speak good English! Where did you learn it?"

For a moment Justin thought the girl would refuse to answer, then she admitted, "My father was American."

Jenny's expression thawed noticeably. "Really! Then you're American like us! That's great!"

The blue eyes suddenly iced over again. "Do not call me American! *This* is my country!"

Justin and Jenny were both bewildered by Estrella's sudden changes of mood. Jenny answered rather coolly, "I just thought . . . I mean, your father . . . does he live here in Bogota?"

Estrella was silent a moment, then she said reluctantly, "I have no father anymore."

"Oh, I'm sorry!" Jenny answered sympathetically. "Does your mother live here, then? Is *she* American?"

Justin saw the cold curtain drop again over Estrella's face. Elbowing Jenny, he whispered, "Don't ask so many questions! You're going to make her mad again!"

Jenny's eyes sparked hot gold, and she elbowed him back. "Look who's talking! You're the one who wants to know who she is!"

Catching Estrella's wide-eyed expression, they both smiled sheepishly, and Jenny asked, "Don't you ever argue with your brothers?"

Estrella looked sadly thoughtful. "I don't have any brothers—or sisters. And my mother died three years ago."

"Oh, that's awful! You aren't . . ." Jenny faltered. "You aren't one of those poor kids living on the street, are you?"

"You don't need to feel sorry for me!" Estrella answered proudly, "I have a new family now—a family of others like myself who have no home of their own."

Again she waved a slender arm around the room. "One day they will take all this gold and give it to those who really need it."

Justin raised unbelieving eyebrows. "Estrella, it would take an army to break in here and take out this gold—if anyone would be dumb enough to try!" He smiled encouragingly. "You're joking, aren't you?"

Her slim back straight as an arrow, Estrella answered firmly, "I am *not* joking! My family are special people. They are freedom fighters, and one day they will free our people from those who take all the wealth and keep it for themselves!"

"Freedom fighters!" Justin repeated in a whisper. He and Jenny stared at each other in horrified understanding. Then Justin demanded doubtfully, "You mean your 'family' are guerrillas? Like the terrorists who threw that bomb and killed all those people yesterday? You can't mean that you're really a member of a guerrilla band!"

Chapter 3

Haunted!

*T*he three children stared at each other for a long moment, then Jenny broke the silence. "You really live with terrorists?" she asked doubtfully. "How can *they* be your family?"

"Don't you dare call my family 'terrorists'!" Estrella's eyes were now the frozen blue of a winter sea. "Yes, they are guerrillas. They work for the freedom of my people. But they are not like those mad men who throw bombs. They would not hurt anyone!"

Jenny looked scornful. "If they are so kind and peaceful, how do they plan on getting all the gold out of here and giving it to the people?"

"I . . . I don't know!" Estrella looked suddenly troubled, but she answered defiantly, "I just know they are good people. They found me on the street with no place to go, and they gave me a home—and food to eat. They even paid for lessons so that I would not forget the language of my father. I am very special for them because no other children are allowed."

She lowered her voice almost to a whisper. "Sometimes,

though, I think it would be nice to have a friend my age, or . . . or perhaps a brother!"

Justin saw sorrow and longing behind the defiance in Estrella's eyes. He put out his hand. "Well, we'll be going back to the United States soon, but we'd sure like to be your friends while we're here!"

Estrella froze, scorn erasing the momentary softness in the blue eyes. She quickly put her hands behind her back. "The United States!" she repeated, her voice dripping with disdain. "What do Americans know about friendship? You are all alike. You pretend to care for people. Then you go away and leave them! Your friendship means nothing!"

Justin was too hurt and puzzled at her reaction to answer, but Jenny demanded angrily, "What do you mean by that? What do you know about Americans?"

"I knew my father!" Catching an astonished stare from a passing tourist, Estrella lowered her voice. "He was an American—like you! He said he loved me, that he would always love me. Then one day he just left. I was only seven years old."

Her voice shook with anger and bitterness. "He never even bothered to write or send money. When my mother died, I would have starved if my 'family' had not found me."

She drew herself up proudly. "No, I don't need any American friends. My 'family' are all the friends I need!"

Jenny bristled with anger. "If you hate Americans so much, why did you stop to talk to us?"

Without waiting for an answer, she turned away. "Come on, Justin! Let's go!"

Justin started to follow, then stopped and said awkwardly, "Well, it was good to meet—" He was interrupted by a shrill whistle, and Steve called from the foot of the stairs, "Hey,

Justin, are you planning on spending the night?'

Justin suddenly realized the lights had dimmed and that they were the only ones left in the vault. Even Estrella had disappeared. He hurried up the stairs. Ahead of him, Steve's clear baritone echoed down the stairwell as he answered Jenny, "So you really like it, huh? Wait till you see Zipaquirá tomorrow. That's even better!"

At the top of the stairs, Justin glanced back. Estrella had stepped out from behind the display case where she had ducked. Perhaps it was only a trick of the light that made the young guerrilla girl look suddenly uncertain and lost as she stared up at them. Catching his glance, she ducked back into the darkness.

"Who's your little friend?" Steve asked as the guard returned his gun and he slid it into a shoulder holster. The rest of their group and even the guide had already left.

Jenny sniffed. "She isn't our friend! She made that pretty clear!"

The short dusk of the tropics had already fallen by the time they left the museum. Like so many fireflies, thousands of office windows twinkled against the black-velvet backdrop of a starless night. In the plaza, underwater floodlights turned the fountains into rainbow-colored cascades of light.

Justin checked his watch. "Only six o'clock and dark already!"

"We're on the equator here," Steve explained. "Days and nights in Colombia are just about exactly twelve hours long. It's light from six A.M. to six P.M. year around."

As they followed Steve across the plaza, the twins told Steve all about the strange girl they had met. As they climbed into the minivan, Jenny concluded, "She wasn't very nice, was she, Justin!"

Justin nodded agreement, but that last glimpse of the young guerrilla girl's troubled face popped into his mind. "Maybe not, but I still feel sorry for her. She . . . I don't think she's very happy."

Jenny sniffed. "Well, we'll never see her again, so I guess it doesn't matter!"

Turning the minivan back onto a major thoroughfare, Steve suddenly asked, "You say she was the one who came over . . . wanted to talk? Are you sure you didn't speak to her first?"

When Justin and Jenny emphatically shook their heads, the young Marine fell silent and seemed lost in thought as they drove back through the rush-hour traffic. As Steve swung the minivan off a traffic-congested overpass, Justin remembered his manners. "Thanks a lot for taking us, Mr. Cardoza."

"Yeah, that was great!" Jenny exclaimed.

"That's my job!" Steve answered. He looked at Justin. "I was telling your sister that I thought we'd head out to the salt mines at Zipaquirá tomorrow. There is less chance of anyone following us if we keep on the move."

There was a twinkle in the dark-brown eyes as he added, "That's a good excuse for sightseeing."

The narrow street was dark and quiet when they arrived back at the embassy guest house, but two American soldiers still stood at attention in the doorway. The four-story building echoed with emptiness as Steve swung open the heavy metal door and ushered the twins into the wide hall. There was no sign of Uncle Pete or Mr. Bascom.

Leading the two children into a gleaming-white kitchen at the rear of the building, Steve lifted the lid of a large pot that simmered on the back of the huge stove. Handing Justin a sack of crusty rolls and a pat of butter, he carried the pot across to a dining room that could seat dozens of people.

"Doesn't anyone else live here?" Justin asked curiously as he looked around the long room with its empty tables.

"Yeah, if this is the American embassy, where are all the people?" Jenny added.

Steve grinned as he dished up three bowls of what he informed them was *sancocho*—a Colombian stew thick with unfamiliar ingredients. "The American embassy is in the center of town—with hundreds of people going in and out all day. This is just a guest house where we house VIPs—Very Important People, that is."

"And *we* are Very Important People?" Jenny asked impishly.

"Let's just say we want to keep you out of trouble," he answered. "At the moment, you Parkers are the only ones here. There are two security guards who double as cooks—if you can call what they do 'cooking'! They are probably upstairs watching TV. And, of course, there are the soldiers on duty outside—though they don't sleep here."

Uncle Pete still had not returned by the time Steve showed the twins up two flights of stairs to where their luggage awaited them in adjoining bedrooms. But late that night, Justin awoke to hear Uncle Pete's familiar whistle from the bedroom next door.

~~~   ~~~   ~~~

The next morning, Justin and Jenny joined Uncle Pete and Steve for breakfast in one corner of the long dining room. One of the security guards was working in the kitchen, and, contrary to Steve's opinion, the cheese omelets were delicious. The twins had already discovered that the "TV" that so absorbed the security guards was actually a series of television screens that kept an eye on every inch of the property.

"How did your meetings go yesterday, Uncle Pete?" Justin asked, wiping his mouth on a napkin.

Uncle Pete set down his coffee cup with a sigh. "Allen Johnson, a young engineer on his first assignment here, was responsible for catching the two men who tried to blow a hole in the pipeline. He deserves a medal for it, but now the guerrilla band these two men belong to are threatening revenge on all our American personnel if we don't release them."

"Are you going to let them go, then?" Jenny asked, her eyes open wide.

"No, we're not. For one thing, the Colombian police have them in custody—not us. Besides, if we gave in to a threat like that, our workers would never be safe again. The terrorists would come back with another threat every time they wanted something."

"What are you going to do, then?" asked Justin.

Uncle Pete leaned back in his chair. "We'll let the Colombian police force take care of the two guerrillas. What happens to them is no businees of ours. But as for Triton Oil, the engineers can't keep their minds on their work if they're worrying about their families. We've decided to pull all our married American executives out of Colombia and replace them with single workers. We'll have to step up security around our bases and office as well."

Catching Jenny's puzzled look, Justin whispered, "That means adding more guards and locks!"

Uncle Pete turned a stern eye on his nephew and niece. "As for you two . . . I want to get you home as soon as possible. I should be done here in a couple of days."

He stood up. "I'll be meeting with the chief of police and our office staff this morning. Steve tells me he has plans for you, so enjoy yourselves and stay out of trouble."

Steve stood up too. "Yeah, I told the kids I'd take them out to Zipaquirá. It's one of the biggest deposits of rock salt in the world—and a lot more!"

"A lot more what?" Justin and Jenny asked at the same time, but Steve just grinned and refused to explain.

A heavy mist blanketed the street outside, and the twins pulled their jackets tight as they waved good-bye to the soldiers on guard duty. An hour later, they had left the last skyscraper behind. Cultivated fields and green pastures wet with fog made a patchwork against low, rolling hills. Fat holstein and jersey cows munched contentedly behind neat barbwire fences. Brick-red farmhouses and barns reminded Justin of last year's vacation in New England.

Bordering the wide, paved highway were mile after mile of long sheds with peaked roofs of translucent green glass. Jenny cried out in delight as she caught sight of a flower stand in front of one shed. The stand was heaped high with carnations, roses, and strange tropical blooms.

"Those are green houses, aren't they!" she said with astonishment. "But why so many? You could grow enough flowers for the whole world in those!"

"Not quite," Steve answered. "But a good portion of the flowers you buy back home in the U.S. are grown in those greenhouses."

Justin had just noticed something more to his liking. A stand at the gate of a prosperous dairy farm annouced in large letters, *Fresas con Crema*. At the bottom of the sign, someone had scribbled for the benefit of tourists: "Strawberries and Cream."

Steve stopped the minivan. "You can't leave Bogota without trying the local strawberries and cream. They're delicious." A few minutes later, Justin and Jenny were nodding agreement over a bowl of oversized strawberries and cream too thick to pour.

The sun had burnt away the mist by the time they were back on the road, and they could now see the mountain range that ringed the high Andes valley. The cone-shaped snowcaps reminded Justin of the steaming peak they had seen from the plane. He told Steve what Uncle Pete had said about the strange peak.

"Yeah, that was quite a disaster! I wasn't in Colombia yet, but there was plenty about it in the news." Steve looked suddenly interested. "You saw steam, eh? Nevada del Ruiz must be simmering again. I hope she keeps a tighter lid on things this time!"

Jenny looked nervously at the ring of snowy mountains. "It . . . it isn't going to erupt again, is it?"

Steve laughed. "There's nothing for you to worry about, Jenny. The Nevada del Ruiz is eighty miles away from Bogota. Besides, the seismologists—those are the scientists who study volcanoes and earthquakes—have been keeping a close eye on that mountain ever since the last eruption. The next time it goes off, everyone will have plenty of warning to get out of the way."

The highway was now winding down out of the vast mountain valley, and they soon left the snowy peaks behind. Palm trees and tropical flowers now mingled with the pine and cypress. Wiping a suddenly damp face, Justin pulled off his jacket. Jenny followed his example.

Noticing their movements without taking his eyes off the road, Steve commented, "Here on the equator, temperatures are pretty much the same all year around. but every time you drop a few hundred feet in elevation, you move into a new climate zone. If we dropped clear to the bottom of these mountains, you'd be in steaming-hot jungle."

Steve himself looked cool and tough in a T-shirt and jeans. Jenny made a face at him. "Do all Marines know as much as you do, Mr. Cardoza?"

"Steve!" he corrected automatically, then grinned. "Well, I do try to read up on all the countries I get stationed in."

A short time later, the winding highway dropped into a small town several centuries removed from the skyscrapers of Bogota. A stone cathedral lifted its weathered spires and arches above low whitewashed homes with the black, wrought-iron balconies and red-tile roofs the twins had noticed in the colonial sections of Bogota. Modern green traffic signs reading *Zipaquirá—Catedral de Sal* pointed their way through narrow cobblestone streets.

"What does *Catedral de Sal* mean?" Justin asked, stumbling over the unfamiliar words. But Steve just shook his head. "You'll see!"

The road ended in a parking lot at the foot of a narrow concrete path that wound its way up a steep hill through cypress groves. As Steve locked the minivan, a long bus with *"Zipaquirá"* emblazoned across both sides pulled up beside them.

Steve and Jenny started up the steep path, but Justin paused to watch an assortment of foreigners—nearly all clad in the international tourist costume of shorts, T-shirt, and camera—pile out of the bus. The few local passengers were easily marked by their dark hair and solemn clothes.

Falling in behind the group of tourists, Justin stopped not far up the path to adjust his own camera. He had just focused the camera on the parking lot, when a car different than any Justin had ever seen roared into the camera frame. Its red body was low and short and round, like an overgrown ladybug.

Snapping a picture, Justin lowered the camera for a better view as the car slammed to a stop at the far end of the parking lot.

Justin was more interested in the strange car than the slim, wiry man who jumped out. He was too far away for Justin to see his face, but his smooth movements and tight jeans gave the impression of youth. Justin hardly noticed the car's passenger until the young man hurried to the other side of the car. Justin caught a glimpse only of a straight back and a long, dark ponytail, as the young man took his passenger by the arm and hurried her off in the opposite direction.

"More locals," Justin thought, losing interest. He hurried to catch up to Steve and Jenny, now far up the path. He caught up with them near a cluster of long, low cement-block sheds and what looked like some sort of mine diggings. Justin guessed that these were the salt mines, but before he could ask, Steve motioned him to move up the path.

The twins had to trot to keep up with Steve's long strides, and both children were out of breath by the time he stopped. They were standing on a wide terrace paved with stone blocks a yard across. To their left was a long, low building. From the brightly covered tables scattered outside, Justin guessed that it was a restaurant. A low wall on their right gave a clear view of the whole valley.

Just ahead, a high wire-mesh gate opened onto a wide, dark opening in the hillside. A loud chatter of different languages echoed like so many tropical parrots as the busload of tourists they had followed up the hill pressed around the ticket stand outside the gate.

Jenny collapsed against the stone wall and wiped her forehead. "Boy, am I out of shape!"

Justin eyed Steve's hard-muscled bare arms respectfully

as the Marine lieutenant hurried over to join the line at the ticket stand. "I'll bet they lift weights in the Marines!"

He propped his elbows on the wide stone wall, then suddenly straightened up. Rubbing the heels of his hands against his eyes, he took another look. "Jenny!" he exclaimed in a low voice. "I think I'm being haunted by girls with long, black hair!"

Chapter 4

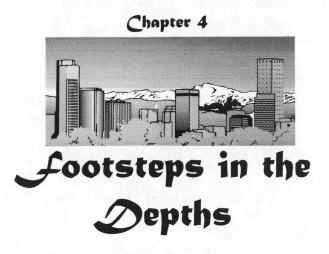

footsteps in the Depths

The low, wide wall on which Justin was leaning ran along the top of the hill they had just climbed. From here he could see the entire valley—the burnt-red roofs and whitewashed walls of the small colonial town, nestled within a surrounding patchwork of green and gold fields. The salt diggings were spread out across the hillside directly below him. Scattered among the mounds of disturbed earth were long, flat ore-cars heaped with what Justin guessed was rock salt.

Leaning further over the wall, Justin rubbed his eyes again. Yes, he was right. In the shade of one of the ore-cars stood a small figure. The heaped-up salt ore cast a shadow across the face, but the long, black ponytail was unmistakable. The girl turned, one arm over her eyes, to study the mountainside above.

"What did you say?" Jenny asked, jumping up to sit on the wall.

"I said I'm being haunted by girls with long, black hair!" Justin repeated.

Jenny sniffed scornfully. "I'd just as soon not be, if they're all as unfriendly as the last one!"

"There she is again. See?"

Dangling her feet over the wall, she followed his pointed finger. "What do you mean? I don't see anyone but tourists!"

Justin looked again. The girl had disappeared. "There *was* a girl standing right there!" he insisted. "She must have ducked behind that cart."

His mind quickly flipped through its memory banks: He saw a young girl petting the white dog that had invaded the guest house; Estrella in the Gold Museum; the girl with a long ponytail who had jumped out of the strange red car. "That's the fourth one!"

"Justin!" Shaking her head with disgust, Jenny said reasonably, "*Most* Colombians have black hair! And at least half of them are girls! And probably a good part of those girls wear their hair long!"

Her explanation was interrupted by a now-familiar whistle, and she jumped off the wall. The rest of the tourists had disappeared. Standing alone outside the wire gate, Steve waved three small pieces of paper in the twins' direction. Jenny hurried across the stone terrace to join him. Still smarting from her sarcasm, Justin followed more slowly, stopping to read the signs warning tourists against rowdy behavior, loudness, and possible cave-ins—printed in English, Spanish, French, and German.

"This is where we go in," Steve informed them as he handed them their tickets. He motioned toward the dark opening in the mountainside. Justin and Jenny followed him out of the bright sunlight to where an impatient guard waited to collect the last tickets. Handing him the slips of paper, both twins looked around in surprise.

Ahead of them, a tunnel wide enough for a dozen people abreast slanted endlessly downward, until it was lost in the inky-black of the mountain depths. Dim lights high above hardly disturbed the darkness, but the rough walls and even the tunnel floor shimmered with a faint light of their own.

The walls were protected by a heavy wire mesh. Justin touched a finger to the grayish-white, quartz-like rock that protruded through the mesh, then cautiously licked the tip of his finger. "Why, it's salt!" he exclaimed.

"That's right," Steve answered. "This whole mountain is made of pure rock salt. Come on! There's plenty more to see."

They hurried after the fast-disappearing group of tourists, their eyes gradually adjusting to the dimness as the sunlight of the entrance dimmed behind them. No one else was in sight now, but once, when their own hollow footsteps paused in front of a statue of a very young angel set into a wire-covered crevice, Justin thought he heard the echo of another pair of feet behind them. But the faint pitter-patter instantly died away, and no one joined them in the bright circle cast by the alcove floodlight.

This place is just plain spooky! Justin told himself as their own footsteps again drowned out any other sound. He stopped again as they came to the first of a series of tunnels that opened up on either side of the main tunnel. Pieces of lumber had been nailed across this opening, but Justin could see it would be easy to crawl over the makeshift barrier.

"Oh, no you don't!" Steve put a hand on Justin's shoulder as he stepped up onto one termite-eaten board to peer into the vast blackness beyond. "Those tunnels are blocked off because they aren't safe anymore. _And_ to keep tourists like you from getting lost—maybe forever!"

"I wasn't going in!" Justin answered hastily. "I was . . . I was just looking."

Justin didn't know how long he had been walking when the tunnel abruptly ended. All three stood still for a long moment, then Justin found his voice. "It's a church! A church built out of salt!"

Steve looked thoroughly pleased with their surprise. "Quite a sight, isn't it! This is the world-famous *Catedral de Sal de Zipaquirá*—'Cathedral of Salt' to you. The only one of its kind in the world!

Opening before them into the sparkling heart of the mountain was a cavern so vast that the scattered busload of tourists seemed lost in its depths. The lights refracted diamond colors off every nodule of salt in the far-flung walls, dazzling their eyes after the dimness of the tunnel. Massive pillars of solid rock salt, gleaming faintly red in the floodlights at their bases, supported a vaulted ceiling so high that it was lost in what looked like star-strewn darkness. Rows of carved wooden benches ran between the pillars.

Above an ornate archway to their right, a trumpeting angel called them to step into his alcove. Grinning at the twins' shouts of wonder, Steve leaned against a salt pillar while Justin and Jenny inspected the shrine inside. Climbing to the top step, Justin suddenly noticed a green glow across the cavern.

"Wait for me!" Jenny ran after him as Justin hurried across the cavern. Reaching the grotto hollowed into the far end of the cavern, Justin was disappointed to discover that it was only a colored floodlight that caused the faint green sparkle of the walls. But he forgot his disappointment in the gentle beauty of the grotto.

A low wooden barrier protected the wide, gleaming steps leading up into the grotto from the dusty shoe marks of countless tourists. Leaning over as far as he dared, Justin saw that the altar, which shimmered the translucent white of pure quartz, was actually carved from one solid block of rock salt. As Jenny took his place at the rail, Justin read the multi-language sign that told how many tons the salt altar weighed.

Sitting down on one of the wooden benches, Justin slowly relaxed in the peaceful quiet of the vast salt cathedral. As he idly watched a flickering light shimmer over the cross that stretched out gold arms above the altar, his mind slipped back to that day at church camp last summer when he first realized how much it had cost Jesus to die on a cross for the sins of the world. That was the day when he and Jenny both had asked Jesus to be their Savior.

Justin didn't know how long he sat there before he realized that the short hairs on the back of his neck were standing straight up. He instantly recognized the prickly sensation. It had always come in useful when Jenny tried to sneak up on him. He turned his head cautiously but saw no one but Steve standing close by, his neck bent back to study a tiny alcove above his head.

Beside him, lost in her own thoughts, Jenny sat watching the green gleam of the floodlights. Justin stood up quietly, and ambled casually over to the altar. Then he whirled around, quickly scanning the width of the cavern. He saw only a few scattered tourists, but the shadow behind one pillar a few yards to the right didn't seem quite natural.

Dodging quickly behind another pillar, he trotted in that direction. But he caught only a slight movement, and the pitter-patter-pitter of running feet disappearing into the shadows.

Jenny was watching him curiously as he returned. "What's wrong?"

"I think we're being followed!" Justin informed her. Then, as she opened her mouth, he added, "And don't tell me it's just my imagination!"

"I wasn't going to!" Jenny answered indignantly. "But really, Justin . . ."

"Justin! Jenny! Come on! There's lots more to see." From a dozen yards away, Steve waved an arm toward the still-unexplored areas of the salt cathedral.

The twins followed Steve toward a far-off, yellow-white beacon. A wooden barrier across the front of a small, well-lit cave brought them to a halt. Here they saw the Christmas story, the crystal-white salt figures radiating light in the beam of powerful floodlights. At one side, Joseph guarded watchfully as Mary bent over the sleeping figure of baby Jesus. Angels proclaimed glad tidings from above, and shepherds knelt in worship at the feet of the baby Savior.

The slight scrape of a tennis shoe against stone echoed loudly in the absolute stillness. Justin whirled around—this time fast enough to catch sight of a thin, pale face just outside the circle of light. Jenny's exclamation told him she had seen the girl's face as well.

"Hey! Why are you following us?" he called. There was a startled gasp and the echo of running feet.

"You go that way!" he whispered urgently to Jenny. "I'll go this way!"

"Hey, kids!" Hardly noticing Steve's call, Justin circled at a run through the salt pillars. Ahead, he caught a glimpse of a slim running figure. Jenny caught up to him just as the running girl darted into a dark opening at the far side of the cathedral.

The twins followed at a trot to discover that the darkness led into a poorly lit cave. The only exit was the opening they had just entered. Against the far wall, the pale beam of the cave's only spotlight full on her face, was the girl they had chased.

"Why, it's Estrella!" Jenny said in astonishment. "Why did you run away from us?" The other girl tensed for flight as the twins walked up to her. Her delicate, pale features seemed thinner than ever with her long hair pulled back into a ponytail.

"That's not the right question!" Justin declared as he casually moved to block any escape. "Ask her why she's been following us!"

He looked at the young guerrilla girl. "You *have* been following us, haven't you?"

Estrella shook her head in a quick no, then—catching Jenny's unbelieving stare—she nodded reluctantly.

"I knew it!" Justin said. He added and subtracted a few memories. "I'll bet that was you in that red car *and* up there on the hillside."

He looked triumphantly at Jenny, then knit reddish-brown eyebrows together. "But why would you want to follow us? And how did you know we were here?"

Justin wondered if he had imagined the sly look in the blue eyes before Estrella lowered long lashes. "I . . . I heard that man you were with at the museum say you would be coming to Zipaquirá today. I . . . I don't often get to speak English . . . I thought it would be good practice."

When Justin and Jenny only stared at her with suspicion, she went on quickly, "No, that isn't true! I didn't come here to practice English. After you left yesterday, I was sorry I had been so unfriendly. I wanted to tell you how sorry I am, so you would not think badly of me. That is why I came."

Still suspicious, Jenny answered coldly, "Why do you want to be friends all of a sudden? We're still Americans, you know!"

Estrella bit her lip and looked away. "Yes, well . . . I was wrong. It is not your fault that you are Americans. And I . . . I think I would like to learn more about my father's country."

Justin broke in. "Then why didn't you just come over and talk to us? Why did you run away?"

Estrella looked wary again. "I was frightened . . . I didn't know how to speak to you. I was afraid you would be angry."

Her voice dropped so low that they had to strain to hear. "I . . . I think I need friends! Will you please forgive me and be my friends?"

Her lower lip quivered, and Justin softened immediately. Holding out his hand, he said gruffly, "That's okay! We all make mistakes!"

Jenny didn't look impressed by the genuine pleading in her voice. "What about your 'family'?" she demanded. "You said they were all the friends you needed!"

Estrella hesitated, then admitted, "They are busy with other things . . . Often they are gone . . . There is no one young."

Straightening her back, she tilted her chin with a touch of her former defiance. "But if you do not wish to forgive, I will go! I will not beg for your friendship! Nor will I tell you the news I have come to give you."

"Jenny!" Seeing Jenny's crossed arms and tightened lips, Justin poked her in the ribs—*hard*. "Remember that verse we learned in Sunday school the week before we left?"

When Jenny looked blank, he added impatiently, "You know! Ephesians 4:32: 'And be ye kind one to another, tender-hearted, forgiving one another, even as God for Christ's sake hath forgiven you.' "

He emphasized each word, and Jenny joined in reluctantly halfway through the verse. As they finished, Estrella said oddly, "You believe in God?"

Jenny looked sheepish. "We sure do. But I guess you'd never know it—the way I've been acting!"

She put out her hand. "I'm sorry! I would like to be your friend."

"What's the big idea running off like that!" Turning, the three children saw Steve's silhouette against the brightness of the cave mouth. His swift strides brought him across the cave to their side. "I've been looking all over for you two!"

Catching sight of Estrella, his eyes narrowed, and he said in the coldest tones Justin had ever heard him use, "You're the girl who was talking to Justin and Jenny yesterday in the museum, aren't you! What are you doing here? Why are you following us?"

"She just wanted to see us again," Justin broke in hastily, surprised by the Marine lieutenant's anger. "She wants to be our friend, and we'd like to be hers!"

"Are you crazy?" Steve exploded. "Have you forgotten who she is?"

He caught Estrella by the shoulder as she started to move away. "So she just happened to show up again today, and she just wants to be your friend! I'll bet she knows a lot more about who you are and what you're doing here than you think! Don't you?"

He addressed the last stern question to Estrella. Twisting away from his grip, she answered defiantly, "Okay, I do know who they are! I have heard on the streets about the two men who were taken by the police, and the man Parker who has come to decide their fate. When they told me of their uncle yesterday, I guessed who they were!"

The young guerrilla girl lifted her chin, wearing what Jenny had called her "princess look" the day before. "I followed them today to say that I was sorry and to be their friend.

It was not hard to know where you would be! You speak very loudly in a crowded place."

As red tinged Steve's bronzed cheekbones, she added, "But I also came because I have heard news that is of great importance to them and to their uncle. If they have told you who I am, then you know that I have ways of finding out things."

"Why would someone like you want to help them?"

Estrella straightened her slim back proudly. "Because they are my friends! They have been kind to me, and I will be kind to them!"

Justin broke in feebly as the Marine lieutenant and the guerrilla girl stared at each other with dislike. "Just a minute, Estrella. What do you mean about Uncle Pete deciding those guys' 'fate'? He doesn't have anything to do with what happens to them! He couldn't free them if he wanted to!"

Ignoring him, Steve demanded coldly. "Okay, what exactly is this helpful news you've got?"

Cutting him off impatiently, Estrella turned to Justin and Jenny. "It does not matter if your uncle can free those men. It is thought that he can, and that is all that matters!"

There was not even the sound of breathing in the small cavern as Estrella added with a dramatic movement of her hand, "I must speak to your uncle! He is in the greatest of danger!"

Chapter 5

Kidnapped!

Sudden loud footsteps startled the entire group. They whirled around to see who was there. Justin was sure he recognized the young man standing just outside the cave mouth as being the driver of the red car he'd seen earlier. Estrella's eyes widened when she saw him, and she whispered urgently, "I can't talk more! I must go!"

Justin protested, "But you can't just go like that! When will we see you again?"

"I will be at the house of Simon Bolivar tomorrow at three o'clock."

Before either Justin or Jenny could say a word, Steve said firmly, "Fine! I'll be there to receive any information you have."

Estrella shook her head. "No! I will speak only to my friends. Bring your uncle and come alone! I will tell him what I know!"

Ducking under Steve's outstretched arm, she darted across the cave floor. By the time Steve and the twins reached the entrance, both Estrella and the young man had disappeared.

There were still parts of the salt caves that they hadn't explored, but Steve had obviously had enough sightseeing. He hurried the twins out of the salt cathedral and up the steep tunnel so quickly that they had to trot to keep up.

Jenny finally broke into Steve's silence. "Steve, what kind of danger could Uncle Pete possibly be in? He didn't have anything to do with those guys! We just got here!"

"Yeah!" added Justin. "Uncle Pete couldn't do anything about those guys anyway! He isn't government or anything!"

"What he can or can't do doesn't matter!" Steve answered grimly without slowing his stride. "Like your friend said, it's what the guerrillas *think* he can do that counts!"

"Well, what *do* they think he can do?" Justin asked, puzzled.

Steve came to a stop. "By threatening Triton Oil property and personnel," he explained patiently, "the guerrillas are trying to force your uncle and the American government to pressure the Colombian police into letting those men go. I'm sure you realize that your uncle has a lot of influence in government circles."

Justin hadn't known this, and he pricked up his ears as Steve continued. "What they don't realize is that both the American and Colombian governments have a rigid policy that they won't give in to threats. If they did, every American citizen abroad would be in danger. Terrorists would take them hostage to force the American government to give in to their demands. So even if your uncle would agree to use his influence to free those men, it wouldn't do any good."

He started walking again. "But the guerrillas don't seem to have gotten that point yet. That's one reason we've got you and your uncle where you are—to keep you safe!"

The twins followed him in silence, but as they neared the entrance, Justin said quietly, "I guess I was pretty stupid, then—telling her our names like that yesterday!"

Steve stopped so suddenly that Justin slid into him. "Now just a minute, Justin! Don't blame yourself. If there was fault, it was mine. I should have warned you not to speak to strangers."

A curious smile lit his bronzed face. "It just never occurred to me you'd find anyone to talk to in a foreign city. Anyway, what's done is done!"

He stode on ahead, nodding to the guard at the entrance, and pushed through the wire gate. The twins fell behind as the brightness of the early afternoon sun dazzled eyes now accustomed to the darkness below. Blinking, Justin commented, "Well, at least Estrella has decided to be our friend. With her help, maybe Uncle Pete can get this cleared up right away."

Jenny frowned. "I don't know. It stills seems pretty strange to me! Why should she go to all this trouble when we've only met her once? She sure changed her mind about being friends in a hurry!"

Justin paused, one hand on the gate. "She explained why she changed her mind. *And* she came all the way out here to warn us about Uncle Pete being in danger. I'd call that pretty nice. Anyway, you promised you'd be her friend!"

Glancing sideways at her brother, Jenny teased, "She's awfully pretty, isn't she!"

Red crept up the back of Justin's neck. "You know that's not it! It's just . . . oh, I don't know!" He shook his head. "There's just something about her . . . I think she really does need friends."

He added, "I mean, look at us! We've got a great family

and lots of friends! I wonder how it would feel to lose it all."

Jenny suddenly looked ashamed. "Yeah, I guess you're right. We did promise to be friends. Anyway, if Uncle Pete really is in danger . . . " She darted across the terrace to where Steve was leaning over the stone wall, waiting for them to catch up. "Steve, we *are* going to meet Estrella tomorrow, aren't we?"

Following Jenny, Justin caught Steve's sudden frown. "I don't know, kids. It could be risky. If this girl knows all about you, who knows how many others do too? Maybe you'd all better sit tight until we can get you out of the country."

Jenny looked like she wanted to argue, but Steve stood up. "We can't decide anything until we've talked to your uncle and Mr. Bascom, so let's get going!"

As they hurried down the winding path, Justin scanned the parking lot below. There was no sign of the little red car or its occupants. He suddenly realized he hadn't told Steve and Jenny about the car, or the driver he'd recognized later in the caverns.

"It must have been a *peta*," Steve decided when Justin finished describing the ladybug-shaped car. "Good work, Justin. That could be a useful piece of information."

Catching their puzzled expressions, he added, "A *peta* is a little turtle—they're shaped just about like one of those cars. A Volkswagen 'bug' we'd call the car in English. They're one of the most popular cars in South America—cheap and easy to fix."

∿ ∿ ∿

Both Uncle Pete and Mr. Bascom, the embassy secretary, were at the guest house when they arrived. Over supper, Steve briefly outlined the events of the last two days. To the twins' surprise, Mr. Bascom seemed very interested in the young guerrilla girl, asking questions until Justin and Jenny had repeated all they could remember of their conversations with Estrella.

When they had finished, Uncle Pete raised his eyebrows at Mr. Bascom. "This whole situation still makes no sense! I can understand this guerrilla band threatening Triton Oil. But how could they possibly know anything about me—or even that I'm in the country?"

Mr. Bascom shrugged. "These groups have ways of getting information. They could have bribed a secretary—or even a janitor—to snoop around the Triton Oil office. Who knows? What matters is that they obviously *do* know about you."

"Yeah, and somehow that information got around to whatever group this girl calls her 'family,' " added Steve. "News travels fast on the street."

He frowned. "Of course, that's assuming this Estrella's telling the truth. I don't trust that girl! Maybe it would be safest just to pretend we never met her . . ."

Mr. Bascom disagreed. "This girl could be a valuable contact for our intelligence gathering bureau. I would certainly like to know what information she has to pass on." He shook his head. "But I don't know that I want to involve the kids."

Steve said thoughtfully, "I could go alone, but I'm sure she wouldn't show unless she saw the kids. Now, if there was some way we could stake out the place . . . That way, if it's a trap . . ."

Uncle Pete slapped a hand against the table. "Now, just a minute! I'm not putting Justin and Jenny in any position where they will run a risk of being hurt!"

The twins had been listening while the adults talked, but Justin couldn't keep quiet any longer. "Uncle Pete, Estrella wouldn't do anything to hurt us! She's our friend! If we don't show up tomorrow, she's going to think we lied when we said we'd be her friend."

Jenny spoke up in support. "I agree with Justin. We did promise to be her friend. Besides, if she does know something, then maybe the police can catch those guys, and Uncle Pete's company can get back to work." She grinned impishly. "Then Steve won't have to baby-sit us anymore!"

"Yeah, if you're in danger, Uncle Pete," Justin added, "we really should find out about it. We don't want anything to happen to you! We just want to talk to her! What could possibly happen?"

Uncle Pete's green eyes twinkled as he looked from one pleading face to the other. "It seems I've heard that from you two before. All right, we'll go. But only if Steve takes the proper security measures."

As Justin and Jenny started to protest, he raised a stern hand. "No, I don't care what this girl said. I'm not taking you anywhere alone!"

"Don't worry!" Steve put in. "I'll hide a couple of guys in the bushes. She won't even know we're there."

～～ ～～ ～～

The next afternoon, Mr. Bascom brought the minivan around to the front door of the guest house. Steve had left an hour earlier with two other Marines whose duty it was to protect the American embassy. As they pulled away from the curb, Justin noticed a group of children playing soccer at the end of the block. *Looks like the same bunch as before, he thought idly.* But he saw no sign of the little white dog.

"I'll drop you off at the entrance," Mr. Bascom told the Parkers as he turned onto a six-lane avenue lined with business offices. "Anyone watching will think you've come alone. You will then leave here with Steve. He should have his men staked out around the grounds by now."

"Do we really *need* to go through all this spy stuff just to talk to a girl?" Justin muttered to Jenny.

"Don't ask me!" Jenny whispered back. "It seems pretty silly!"

From the driver's seat, Mr. Bascom said sternly, "We've learned the hard way here in Bogota not to take any chances!"

"Exactly what *is* this house of Simon Bolivar?" Uncle Pete put in quickly, as the twins flushed with embarrassment.

With a smile, Mr. Bascom looked back at the two children. "Can either of you tell us who Simon Bolivar was?"

Justin answered hesitantly, "Wasn't he the guy who helped South America get its independence from Spain? Like George Washington back home?"

"That's right!" Mr. Bascom nodded approvingly. "He was also the first president of Colombia. We are going to his family mansion here in Bogota. It's now open to the public."

Leaving the office buildings behind, he drove through a wide intersection, then pulled to a stop half-way through the next block. Jumping out onto a broad cement sidewalk, Justin looked both ways as the embassy minivan drove off. There was little traffic at this hour of the afternoon, and no one else shared the sidewalk as far as he could see.

Above Justin's head, an untrimmed cypress tree leaned over a weathered stone wall to run feather green fingers through his hair. Justin followed Jenny and Uncle Pete to the heavy metal gate that swung between tall stone pillars. As Uncle Pete dug the small entrance fee from his pocket, the usual guard handed tickets through a barred stone window and swung open the gate.

The gentle, green oasis on the other side of the gate was unexpected, and as the click of the heavy latch shut out the bustle of the city, Justin felt that he had stepped back into another, quieter century. Even the roar of distant traffic was cut off by the gentle rush of wind through the evergreens.

The three Parkers walked through a maze of oddly cut yew hedges that bordered a series of spouting fountains, stone statues, and small ponds where goldfish glinted in the afternoon sun. Tucked into odd corners, and blazing from formal, carefully tended beds, were the flowers whose colors splashed across the garden like a child's spilled paint box.

Justin paused to look across the maze of green. It was a warm weekday afternoon. The only visitor in sight was a middle-aged tourist taking pictures of the flowers. If Steve and the other security agents were somewhere in the mass of shrubbery, they were too well hidden to be seen from where Justin stood. The idea of terrorists and danger suddenly seemed ridiculous.

Uncle Pete stopped in front of the square, two-story mansion at the far end of the garden. The usual burnt-red tiles of the roof contrasted with the blinding white of the old adobe walls. Flower pots nodded colorful heads from the black iron balconies overhead. Glancing at his watch, he announced, "Three o'clock on the dot. Do you see any sign of your friend?"

Justin shook his head reluctantly, and Jenny suggested, "Maybe she's inside. Why don't we take a look?"

"Good idea," Uncle Pete agreed. "If she doesn't show, you'll get a history lesson out of the afternoon, at least."

As they filed through the tiled entryway, Justin discovered that the entire house was wrapped around a large courtyard. In the center, a few stunted citrus trees in pots sheltered another fountain. High pillars held up a verandah that circled the courtyard. In its shade, rows of hand-carved doors opened into high-ceilinged, whitewashed rooms. Heavy ropes across the open doors kept visitors from entering.

There was no sign of a guide or Estrella. *Maybe she's just late,* Justin thought as he followed Jenny and Uncle Pete along the verandah. Although a small part of his mind stayed alert for the tell-tale prickle at his neck that would inform him of spying eyes, he decided to enjoy the tour.

He peered over Jenny's shoulder into a room that was once a study. The room looked as though the nineteenth-century liberator had just stepped out for an afternoon stroll.

One corner of the verandah opened into a long room where finely embroidered chairs, imported from France a century before, sat around highly polished tables. Paintings by famous European artists looked down from the walls, and a crystal chandelier hung unlit from the mural-covered ceiling.

In every room, treasures of china and silver peered out of locked glass cases. Justin and Jenny followed Uncle Pete up one of the broad, tiled staircases that curved up to the second floor from each corner of the courtyard. Here too, a row of carved-wood doors opened onto a wide balcony that circled the courtyard.

Justin whistled as he pointed out a four-poster bed with a faded silk canopy in the master bedroom. "Look how small that bed is! People must have been awfully short back then."

Reading a sign printed as usual in several languages, Justin mentally translated the centimeters to inches. "Wow! That guy was only four feet ten inches tall!"

Jenny giggled at a set of the liberator's clothes preserved in a glass case. "*I* couldn't even get into those."

As the two children followed Uncle Pete down the far staircase, Justin paused again to scan the courtyard. "I wonder what's keeping Estrella!"

"Maybe she never meant to come," Jenny suggested idly,

leaning over the rail to watch a pair of bright-yellow birds. "Maybe she was just pulling our leg."

Justin bristled. "Don't be ridiculous! There could be a hundred reasons why she's late."

"Let's get a move on, kids!" Uncle Pete was waving at them from the top of a stairway that led below ground. Forgetting their argument, the twins hurried to catch up and followed Uncle Pete down toward the servants' quarters and kitchen.

They entered a vast underground chamber dimly lit by a few barred windows high on the wall. Copper utensils and ladles hung from its low rafters. Brick ovens built into the earthen walls were stil blackened with a century or two of soot, and a rusty, three-legged pot was perched in a fireplace large enough to roast an entire ox. A heavy iron spit showed that it had probably been used for that very purpose.

As they emerged back into the afternoon light, Uncle Pete glanced at his watch. "Well, kids, it doesn't look like your friend is going to show. This has been an interesting outing, but I have work waiting."

"Yeah, let's go home!" Jenny agreed. "She's obviously not coming!"

"Can't we wait just a little longer?" Justin begged, scanning the courtyard one last time. "We might not get another chance to find out what she knows."

Uncle Pete shook his head firmly. "It's already four o'clock. If she planned to show, she would be here by now. Come on. We'll try to locate Steve and get a ride home."

In the tiled entryway, the twins used the last of the savings they had brought along for the trip to buy a covered silver sugar bowl—supposedly a copy of Simon Bolivar's, and incredibly low in price. Silver was plentiful and still quite cheap in Colombia, Uncle Pete explained.

Trailing a few feet behind as they threaded back through the maze of walkways that led to the gate, Justin saw with disappointment that the garden was empty. Even the solitary tourist was gone, and if Steve and the other agents were there, they were well hidden.

"Justin! Jenny!"

Justin instantly recognized the cool, precise girl's voice. Pointing, he announced triumphantly, "Look! I told you she'd come."

Dark-shaded blue eyes were peering through the grill-work of the iron gate, then a slim arm waved through the opening. Justin and Jenny hurried to the gate, Uncle Pete close behind. "Estrella, where were you?" Justin demanded. "We were just about to leave!"

What they could see of Estrella's expression looked uneasy. "I . . . I could not buy the ticket to get in. I have been waiting here for you to come out."

Uncle Pete bent down to look through the grill work. "Kids, would you introduce me to your friend?"

"Oh, yes." Jenny turned hurriedly to Uncle Pete. "Uncle Pete, this is Estrella. Estrella, this is my uncle that you wanted to talk to."

Uncle Pete studied the slim, pale features closely. "If you want to talk to me, come on in. We'll take care of your ticket."

They could see Estrella shake her head, then she stepped out of sight. "No, I can't let you do that," her voice floated stubbornly from the other side of the gate. "If you wish to hear what I have to say, you must come out here and speak with me."

Uncle Pete glanced around the garden, and Justin guessed that he was looking for some sign of Steve. "All right," he said at last, looking exasperated.

Pushing open the gate, the three Parkers stepped out onto the sidewalk. Justin looked up and down the street. It was empty of pedestrians, and the only traffic was a long, black Mercedes Benz limousine moving in their direction a couple of blocks away.

"Hi, Estrella! We thought you weren't coming!" Estrella looked surprised at Jenny's quick hug, but she hugged her back and shook Justin's outstretched hand.

"Estrella, I'm glad to meet you, but we can't stay here long." Uncle Pete looked down kindly at the young guerrilla girl. "Why don't you go ahead and tell me what you have to say—*and* how you learned about us."

Moving away from the twins, Estrella stared up at Uncle Pete. Her speech sounded rehearsed as she answered calmly, "I hear many things in the street. When Justin and Jenny told me their names, I knew who you were. They were kind to me and promised to be my friends, so I decided to help them."

Her voice died away as she glanced up the street. Justin followed her gaze, but saw nothing but the black limousine now only a block away. Uncle Pete's big foot tapped impatiently, but he repeated gently, "Well, what is it that you heard?"

Estrella opened her mouth, but her voice was suddenly drowned out by the loud gunning of an engine. Startled, Justin looked up to see the Mercedes Benz now hurtling down the street toward them. The mirror-like one-way glass of the windows hid any sign of a driver. As it neared the four on the side walk, the limousine suddenly braked and a rear window slid down.

Justin glimpsed a black hood and a gloved hand clutching an egg-shaped object. Then, as a black, leather-clad arm reached through the window and made a smooth overhand toss, Estrella shouted, "Run!"

Justin instinctively jerked away as she grabbed at his jacket and caught Jenny by the hand, and she hissed, "Don't be stupid!"

With more strength than they would have guessed possible, the young guerrilla girl shoved Justin and Jenny away from the car. Stumbling back against the stone wall, Justin watched as the egg-shaped object tumbled end over end through the afternoon sun. From the corner of his eye, he saw Estrella cover her head with her arms. Then, with a blast of thunder, his world exploded!

Chapter 6

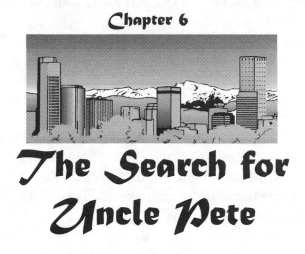

The Search for Uncle Pete

Justin lay unmoving, one cheek against the cement pavement where the explosion had thrown him. His lungs felt deflated. He vaguely sensed that someone lay beneath him, but he couldn't move. Lifting his head cautiously, he choked as a sharp odor and dust rushed into his lungs.

Several yards beyond the gate, dust and black smoke drifted up from a gaping hole in the stone wall. Chunks of concrete and shattered stone littered the sidewalk. *How could they possibly have missed us?* he wondered numbly. Then, as he blinked the dirt and debris from his eyes, he again felt his breath snatched away.

The rear door of the black limousine stood open, and a tall, hooded figure all in black was shoving Uncle Pete into the back seat. Another slim, black-hooded figure—Justin couldn't tell whether it was a man or a woman—scanned the sidewalk, while balancing a machine gun with an obviously experienced hand.

Justin tried to shout, but his voice came out in a squeak.

Before he could even move, the first hooded figure had climbed in beside Uncle Pete. The one with the machine gun slammed the door shut and jerked open the front door. The door was still open when the engine roared and the Mercedes Benz moved smoothly away from the curb.

"Justin, you're squashing me!" a muffled voice gasped from beneath him. "Get off!"

Justin rolled over and struggled to his feet just as the heavy gate in the stone wall clanged open and Steve ran out, followed by the other two Marines. *Nice of you to show up now*! Justin thought savagely, before he realized that no more than a minute had gone by since they first stepped out the gate.

Holding an army-caliber pistol high with both hands, the Marine lieutenant took in the scene with one glance. Dropping into a crouch, he brought the pistol down expertly to bear on the black limousine. But whatever he planned to do, it was too late. Still picking up speed, the Mercedes Benz was already far down the block.

It had all happened so quickly that Justin stood unmoving, staring down the street in frozen dismay. Part of his mind registered Jenny and Estrella struggling to their feet behind him. Grabbing his arm, Jenny cried out, "What happened? Where's Uncle Pete?"

Justin motioned hopelessly after the speeding car, which at that instant turned a corner and disappeared. The other two security agents had dropped their guns. One was shouting into a walkie-talkie while the other scanned the debris. Steve walked back toward them, frustration all over his bronze features.

"Okay, kids!" he snapped. "What happened? Where is Mr. Parker?"

Jenny was looking around in a daze, one hand rubbing

sudden tears from her dust-covered cheeks. She choked, "I . . . I don't know! They took him away!"

Putting an arm around his sister, Justin got out an answer. "Some men in that big, black car—I saw them throw the bomb. Then they shoved Uncle Pete in the back and took off."

Justin's arm dropped as Jenny moved away to stand in front of Steve. Looking angrily up at the broad-shouldered Marine, she demanded, "Why did you let them get Uncle Pete? You said you were watching us! You said we'd be safe!"

"You *were* safe!" Steve snapped an answer. "Inside that gate! Why did you leave the property? Don't you have any sense?"

"Estrella called us out," Justin explained wearily. "She wouldn't come in. We didn't think a few minutes would hurt anything."

Steve seemed to notice the young guerrilla girl for the first time. He looked down at the dirt-streaked face, then with cold anger, "I might have known you'd be in on this!"

Estrella looked just as angry as the Marine lieutenant. Turning to Justin, she stormed, "Why is he here? I told you to come alone!"

"I was the one who insisted on coming. I was sure you weren't to be trusted. And I was right, wasn't I?" Steve caught Estrella by the shoulders. "You planned this, didn't you! You're in more trouble than you've ever been in your life."

Justin caught a look of fear in the blue eyes as Estrella protested, "I know nothing of this, I swear! I stayed outside because I had no money for the ticket."

She turned to the twins. "You tell him."

"We'll see!" Steve muttered as Justin and Jenny nodded agreement. Estrella looked faintly triumphant when Steve checked her pockets and found them empty. "You see? It was of this danger that I came to warn you. Those were the men who wanted to harm your uncle."

Steve was still angry. "Didn't you look around, girl? Those men probably followed you all the way here!"

Estrella pulled herself up proudly. "Don't blame me! How do you know they didn't follow you? It wouldn't be hard to find out where you are staying!"

Justin had a sudden mental picture of the band of children outside the embassy guest house. He raised his hands to his still-ringing ears, suddenly exhausted and desperately wishing he could shut out the angry voices. "Who cares whose fault it was! They've got Uncle Pete! We've got to get him back!"

He dropped his hands back to his side and turned to Steve. "Estrella couldn't have anything to do with this. She saved our lives when that guy threw the bomb. If it's anyone's fault, it's ours for going outside the gate."

Steve looked suddenly tired, the anger draining from his face. "I'm sorry. kids. I've no right to yell or to blame anyone. It's just that this was supposed to be such a simple operation."

A siren interrupted him, and moments later the street was crowded with army vehicles and Colombian soldiers. With the ease of much practice, a pair of military police threw up a heavy rope along the sidewalk. One of the Marines hurried over, holding out a few glinting fragments. "Looks like an Army-issue grenade they threw!"

Steve nodded agreement as he glanced over the fragments, then led the three children away from the roped-off area. Justin saw the dark-blue embassy minivan screech to a halt behind a police jeep. Mr. Bascom climbed down, and Steve hurried over to talk to him.

As Justin slumped against the stone wall to wait, he noticed for the first time the painful sting of his face and hands. Wiping the grit from his skinned palms against his jeans, he touched one cheek cautiously. His fingers came away red-stained, and he realized that he must have scraped it against the concrete pavement when the blast sent him flying.

As the two girls came over to stand beside him, he noticed that Estrella was limping and that the knees of her worn jeans were torn and red-stained. Jenny had a long scrape down one arm. Their hair and clothes were as coated with chalky dust as his own.

"Kids!" Justin stood up as Steve waved the children over to the minivan. "Dave and Mac will take care of the local police." He indicated the other two security agents who were talking with a Colombian army officer inside the roped-off area. "Mr. Bascom and I are taking you back to the guest house."

As the twins climbed into the back of the van, Steve looked down at Estrella, who stood alone on the pavement, looking very dirty and a little lost. He added without his former anger, "You too! We'll have a few questions to ask you."

The rest of the day had the unreal quality of a bad dream. Mr. Bascom kindly refrained from asking any questions until the three children had all bathed and changed—Jenny lending Estrella a spare pair of jeans and T-shirt—and Steve had administered basic first aid to their cuts and scrapes.

Only when they were drinking the last of another pot of Colombian *sancocho* did Mr. Bascom take Steve and the three children, step by step, over every detail of what had happened since he had dropped the Parkers off earlier in the afternoon.

When they finished, Mr. Bascom said heavily, "Well, kids, I can't tell you how sorry I am about this. Be sure that we will be doing all we can to get your uncle back."

Running long fingers through his receding tight curls, he eyed Estrella sharply. "So you knew something like this might happen?"

"I heard that there were men who wanted to capture Justin and Jenny's uncle—to keep him until you let your prisoners go. It was for this reason that I came today." Estrella shrugged. "I am sorry that I was too late."

Justin's mind seemed to clear for the first time since the kidnapping. He said thoughtfully, "Those guys who took Uncle Pete must have been from that guerrilla band who tried to bomb the oil line—the ones who have been threatening Triton Oil. Well, you've got two of their guys in prison. Maybe they'd know where those guerrillas might have taken Uncle Pete!"

Mr. Bascom looked approvingly at Justin. "That's good thinking. You can be sure the Colombian police are going to be questioning those two men pretty thoroughly."

He looked down at the young guerrilla girl. "What about you, Estrella? Can you think of any place they might have taken Mr. Parker—or anyone who might be able to find out?"

Estrella nodded. "I will do all I can to help find my friends' uncle. I have many ways of finding things out."

She added hesitantly, "But there is one thing. I . . . my 'family' left the city today. I . . . I stayed behind to warn my friends. I don't know where I will stay."

Justin spoke up immediately. "Well, I'm sure you can stay with us. Can't she, Mr. Bascom? . . . Steve? . . . I mean, she stayed behind just to warn us."

His back to the children, Steve leaned over and spoke quietly to Mr. Bascom. Justin barely caught Mr. Bascom's soft answer. "It might be the best way to keep an eye on her."

Steve nodded to the waiting children. "You're certainly welcome to stay, Estrella. We'll appreciate any help you can give us."

Still pink around the eyelids, Jenny had been staring down at her empty bowl. But at this, she looked up and smiled at the young guerrilla girl. "She can sleep with me. I've got plenty of extra clothes—even an extra toothbrush."

Estrella nodded satisfaction. "That is good. Then I will go out now and see what news I can find. I will be back to-night to sleep."

"Oh, no you don't!" Steve suddenly stood up. "No one is going in or out of this building except myself and Mr. Bascom. We aren't taking any more risks. If Estrella is really anxious to help, she can just tell me what she knows and I'll check it out myself!"

His expression was so discouraging that Estrella didn't argue. She said glumly, "If that is what you wish! But I can't promise that my friends will speak with you."

Mr. Bascom rose to his feet as the security guard Justin had seen in the kitchen that morning came in to collect their empty dishes. "Well, kids, I don't think there is anything more we can do right now. Steve, why don't you write down any contacts or information Estrella can give you and begin work-ing on that. Justin and Jenny . . ."

As he paused, Justin suddenly realized that what he wanted most in the world right now was to talk to his parents. As usual, Jenny echoed his thoughts. "Mr. Bascom, could we please call Mom and Dad?"

"Just what I was going to suggest." Mr. Bascom again ran his fingers through his tight, black curls and sighed. "I imagine they'll want you on the first plane home."

Leaving Estrella and Steve bent over a notebook, he led

the twins to the next room and showed them how to dial the international area code.

"You go first!" Jenny told Justin. "You're better at explaining."

Justin waited impatiently as the dial tone buzzed in his ear, then sighed with relief as he heard his mother's warm voice say, "This is the Parker residence."

But his relief turned to dismay as the voice went on, "We are unavailable at the moment. Please leave your name and number after the beep."

His father's voice suddenly broke into the taped message, "Pete, Justin, Jenny—if you should call, we'll be back in a few days. I managed to finish that project sooner than expected, and Helen and I decided to get away . . ."

As his father's voice continued, Justin looked blankly at Mr. Bascom. "They went camping! It . . . it's just the answering machine. They won't be home for three more days!"

Mr. Bascom took the phone from Justin and spoke crisply into the receiver, "Mr. and Mrs. Parker, this is Mr. Marvin Bascom from the American embassy in Bogota. Your children are fine, but we would appreciate you getting in contact with us at your earliest convenience. Our phone number is . . ."

He rattled off a line of numbers, then hung up. Turning to the twins, he explained, "We need to get hold of them as soon as possible, but I didn't want them thinking something has happened to you."

Justin slumped into a chair. He hadn't realized how much he had counted on hearing his parents' reassuring voices. "What do we do now?" he asked.

"We'll keep you here under guard until we hear from your parents," Mr. Bascom answered firmly. "Then you'll be on the first plane home—with or without your uncle!"

Dropping into another chair, Jenny said hesitantly, "But . . . but you'll have found him by then, won't you?"

Mr. Bascom faced the two children squarely. "Look, I'm going to be honest with you. We could find your uncle in a couple of days. But Colombia is a big country. We don't even know if your uncle is still in Bogota. Sometimes it takes months to recover a hostage taken by guerrillas. Sometimes . . ."

He broke off, and Justin finished for him, "Sometimes you never get them back!"

Justin jumped to his feet. "Sometimes they kill them, don't they? They could be hurting Uncle Pete right now!"

Mr. Bascom patted him on the shoulder. "Don't worry, Justin. I'm sure your uncle is just fine. They won't hurt him as long as they hope to trade him for their two men in prison. And by the time they realize the government won't trade . . ."

He hesitated, then went on, "Well, we'll just have to make sure we've found him by that time."

Estrella came into the room just then, followed by Steve, who seemed very satisfied with the scribbled notes he was reading over. A short time later, the three children climbed the stairs to their rooms. Justin joined the girls in Jenny's room as Jenny showed Estrella the extra twin bed and dug out a spare sweat suit.

It wasn't yet their usual bedtime, but as Justin stretched out on Jenny's bed, he realized how tired and sore he was. Echoing his thoughts, Jenny gave a mouth-splitting yawn. Estrella smiled slightly. "It would be well if we went to sleep. There is nothing more we can do tonight."

At her words, Justin suddenly straightened up. "Oh, yes there is!"

He looked at his sister and knew she'd had the same

thought. Estrella paused with one hand on the bathroom door as Jenny scrambled over to sit by Justin. She stood there un-moving as Justin and Jenny bowed their heads and, first one, then the other, prayed that God would protect Uncle Pete, wherever he was, and bring him safely back.

When they had finished, Estrella asked curiously, "Do you really think God is going to hear your prayers?"

The twins looked at each other again and smiled for the first time that evening. Justin answered, "We *know* He does!"

"Carlos says that God is an invention of the rich and pow-erful to keep the poor under their thumb," Estrella remarked, still with her hand on the doorknob. "If the poor pray to God for help, they will not think to fight those who are oppressing them."

But she spoke thoughtfully rather than with scorn, and as she left the room, she added, "I once knew someone who spoke about God as you do."

Much later, Justin lay awake, staring into the darkness above his bed. Tiredness pressed on his eyelids, but his mind would not stop going over and over the events of the after-noon. He was envying the two girls sleeping peacefully next door when a light tap at the door startled him into sitting up.

"Justin, are you awake?" he heard his sister whisper. He felt a weight settling on the far end of the bed.

"Yeah, I'm awake!" he whispered back. "You couldn't get to sleep either?"

He felt her shake her head. "No. I've been thinking and thinking!"

Giving up any attempt to sleep, Justin asked, "Yeah? What about?"

"Justin, I've been wondering," Jenny said, still in a whis-per, "Do you think it could really have been Estrella who brought those guerrillas to kidnap Uncle Pete?"

"What?" Justin sat up, his exclamation almost a shout.

"Shh!" Jenny hissed, then added, "Well, what if Steve was right! I mean, don't you think it's strange that those guer-rillas showed up right after Estrella called us out of the gate?"

"No, I don't!" Justin answered flatly, reaching over to switch on a lamp that stood on a wooden table beside the bed. Jenny blinked at the sudden light as he demanded, "Have you forgotten she saved our lives when that grenade went off?"

A knock at the door startled them into silence. The door opened, and Estrella looked in. "I woke to find Jenny gone. Is there something wrong?"

As Justin and Jenny quickly shook their heads, Estrella joined them on the twin bed. Drawing her knees up to her chin, she wrapped her arms around them and said hesitantly, "I am sorry that you cannot sleep. I too am very sad about your uncle. I wish I had never asked you to meet me . . ."

Throwing a glance at Jenny, Justin interrupted gruffly, "It wasn't your fault, Estrella! Anyway, we sure appreciate the way you're helping us get him back."

"*If* we ever get him back!" Jenny said, wiping at suddenly overflowing tears. "Oh, Justin, what if we never . . ."

"Justin! Jenny! Please do not be so sad!" Even Jenny could not mistake the genuine sympathy in Estrellas's voice. She jumped off the bed. "Please do not cry, Jenny. You must not worry! Your uncle *will* come back to you soon. I promise you! I, Estrella, will find him myself!"

Chapter 7

I Found Him!

Justin and Jenny stared at Estrella in surprise. Jenny demanded, "How are you going to do that? You're not even allowed to leave the building!"

Estrella looked scornful. "Do you really think they can keep me here if I want to leave?"

Justin thought of the locked, heavy metal doors, and the surveillance cameras he had seen in the halls. He said slowly, "I don't see how you can possibly get out. You know they'll just stop you if they see you."

"There are ways," Estrella answered vaguely. She added sharply, "I must get out. No matter what Steve says, the people I have told him of will not speak to him as they will to me."

"Well, why don't you tell Steve that," Jenny said reasonably. "Maybe he could take you along with him or something."

"No!" Estrella shook her head sharply. "If they saw that I did not come alone, they would not speak to me, either."

"I still think you should talk to Steve," Jenny argued. "It

could be dangerous for you out there."

"No, I will not talk to that man again! You know he doesn't like me. He would just try to stop me. Besides, there is no one trying to kidnap me! Why should I be caged up here like a prisoner?"

Estrella looked from one to the other. "If you want your uncle back, you must promise to keep quiet—or I will not be able to help you."

Jenny opened her mouth to argue further, but Justin, wearily rubbing his eyes, interrupted, "Let her try, Jenny! We've got to do anything we can to help Uncle Pete. Anyway, it's time we all get back to bed!"

"Good! Tomorrow I will see what I can find out!" Estrella started toward the door, and Jenny reluctantly followed her. Turning out the light, Justin soon fell into a troubled sleep.

≈   ≈   ≈

There was no further news about Uncle Pete the next morning, and the next three days settled into a pattern of waiting. Steve was often gone, and when he was there, he was usually on the phone or sifting through the pile of reports that a Colombian police officer dropped off twice a day.

It was noon on the first day when Mr. Bascom informed the three children that the embassy had received a ransom note. "We were right. It's the same group that threatened your uncle's company. They want to exchange him for their two members in prison."

"What are you going to do?" Justin asked.

"There's nothing we can do," Mr. Bascom answered grimly. "You know the government policy about giving into kidnappers."

As he left the room, Jenny turned to Estrella and said desperately, "Estrella, you've got to find him soon!"

Estrella squeezed her hand sympathetically. "Don't worry! I will find him in time."

Estrella often slipped away, but she was never gone long and managed to be there every time Steve or Mr. Bascom reported any updates on the search for Uncle Pete. As they had promised, the twins said nothing about her occasional disappearances. But Justin couldn't restrain his curiosity.

The afternoon after the kidnapping, Justin decided to try to leave the building for himself. He made his way through darkened hallways down to the basement, but was still yards from the back door when a security guard tapped him on the shoulder.

"You don't want to go out there!" the guard said, kindly but firmly.

"I didn't really want to go out, I just wanted to see if I could do it without being caught," Justin answered with a grin. He gave up trying to figure out how Estrella managed to leave the guest house undetected.

The twins discovered that the security guards' row of surveillance screens weren't the only TV sets in the guest house. They located a large recreation room on the third floor. Here, the security guards relaxed when they were off duty. Occasionally joined by Steve, Mr. Bascom, or one of the guards, the three children spent most of their time there—reading magazines, playing board games, deciphering the Spanish news broadcasts on the big-screen TV, or just talking.

It was after Justin's attempt to defeat the security system, as the three children huddled on the floor over an antique Monopoly game, that Justin suddenly remembered something. Glancing up from a pile of paper money, he asked, "Estrella, who's Carlos?"

When Estrella looked up in surprise, he added, "You

know . . . you mentioned him last night."

"Yes, I had forgotten I said his name." Estrella hesitated, then went on. "Carlos is the leader of my 'family.' It was he who found me on the streets—he made me a part of his band."

Looking up from the board, Jenny asked curiously, "How old were you when you joined this band?"

Estrella dropped her paper money. To Justin's surprise, she answered readily. "I was nine years old the day Carlos found me on the street. I remember very well . . . I was looking at a magazine I found in a barrel. I was cold and hungry— I had been hungry for so long! To forget my stomach, I was reading out loud the words I knew on the page. Then Carlos spoke to me. He took me to a *panaderia*—a bakery."

Estrella suddenly smiled, her completely charming smile that the twins had seen so seldom. "I remember that I ate so much I was sick! But he was not angry. He spoke to me other days, and one day he took me to meet his band."

She spread her hands out. "And that is all! I have been part of his 'family' ever since. Perhaps someday you will meet them and see how kind they are."

Jenny had lost interest in the Monopoly game. In a rapidfire series of questions, she demanded, "Where did you go after Carlos took you to meet his band? Do all your 'family' live together? How many are there? Do you go to school?"

When Estrella seemed reluctant to answer, she pleaded, "Come on, Estrella! We've told you all about us. Now we'd like to hear about you!"

When Justin added his persuasion, Estrella continued. "Well, I told you that my 'family'—Carlos—paid that I might better learn my father's language. Carlos took me to a school. I studied English and all the other things children study in school—writing, arithmetic, science. I lived there for a long time—with many other girls who did not have families close by."

"It sounds lonely," Jenny commented.

"I had food to eat and a place to sleep!" Estrella answered. "That is what matters. And Carlos came often to take me to visit the rest of my 'family.' "

Seeing that the twins still looked interested, she went on. "They have a big house. I do not know how many there are—perhaps a dozen, perhaps twenty. They come, they go. They have important things to do. When I grew bigger, Carlos let me do things for them—carry messages sometimes, translate English words, speak to . . ."

She broke off suddenly, and Justin added curiously, "Well, I guess that *was* pretty nice of them to do all that for you. But aren't you awfully young to be a guerrilla? You're no older than we are. Didn't you say there weren't any other children in your 'family'?"

"Yes, I am the only one," Estrella answered proudly. "Children are not allowed in the freedom fighters. But I am *special* . . . their—how do you say it in English?—their mascot."

Jenny looked puzzled. "I still don't understand! Steve says there's thousands of kids who live in the streets. What made them pick *you* for their band?"

"Because she speaks English," Justin commented idly as he put away the Monopoly board. He looked up as Estrella's hand froze in mid-air. "I mean, it must be pretty useful!"

Forgetting the scattered pair of dice she was reaching for, Estrella said in a whisper, "It *was* an English magazine! I remember now. Carlos asked me how I knew the words."

She jumped up. "No, it was not because of that! They are kind . . . they care about me. I am glad to use my English to help them!"

At that moment the door swung open and Mr. Bascom walked in, ending their conversation. The twins scrambled to their feet, eagerly asking if he had any news for them.

Mr. Bascom looked serious as he shook his head. "And I'm afraid the Colombian police haven't been able to get any information out of those two prisoners. If they do know where this bunch is hiding out, they sure aren't telling!"

Mr. Bascom asked if Justin and Jenny had heard from their parents yet, and when they glumly admitted they hadn't he left again abruptly. None of the children felt like playing games or talking after that, so they decided on an early bed-time.

On the second morning, Justin looked up from a battered checkerboard as he caught a familiar name. A shot of a steaming, snowcapped peak filled the TV screen. Estrella wasn't there to translate, so he called over to Steve, who was leafing through that day's newspaper. "Hey, Steve, isn't that the mountain we saw spouting steam? The one that erupted and buried that town?"

"The Nevada del Ruiz," Steve confirmed, lowering the paper. "It sounds like it's going to do more than spout steam! They're warning of another eruption any day."

Studying Jenny's red checkers with care, Justin said idly, "I meant to ask you before—how could that mountain do so much damage? I mean, I can see a volcano burning up a town. But you'd think you could just climb out of the way of melting snow!"

"Justin, I don't think you've got the picture. I remember watching that disaster on the news." Steve folded up the paper before continuing. "Just imagine literally hundreds of tons of snow melting from the heat of that eruption. You've got as much water as the Niagara Falls rushing down the mountain canyons, scraping away dirt and boulders and trees . . . carrying it all down into the valleys. It's called *lahar*—that mixture of ice, mud, rock, you name it.

"By the time the *lahar* reached Armero, it was a river of sticky mud and rock forty feet high . . . that's taller than most of the buildings. Most people were sound asleep when that mud slide swept over the town. I saw the pictures—you couldn't even see the church steeple!"

"Oh, that's awful!" Jenny shuddered as she absently moved a checker piece. "What's going to happen this time? Are they going to move all the people?"

"They won't need to evacuate this time," Steve reassured her, listening closely to the rest of the news clip. "They say this will be a fairly small eruption, and the seismologists can tell exactly how the snowcap will melt. The only thing up that way are uninhabited mountain gullies. Hikers are being warned to stay out of the area. The mud will probably catch a few wild animals and lost cattle, but that's all."

Just then Justin took advantage of Jenny's lack of concentration to jump her last four checkers. Jenny's cries of indignation quickly drove the news story from their thoughts.

Estrella came in a short time later. After a short talk with her about his scribbled notes, Steve left the guest house. Estrella showed no signs of going out again, but as one of the security guards had decided to spend the afternoon with them in the lounge, the twins were unable to ask her if she had made any progress.

After supper, Jenny and Estrella were alone again in the lounge—Estrella was translating the international news for Jenny—when Justin walked in and tossed a newspaper onto the coffee table. "Hey, look what the guard gave me!"

Jenny and Estrella quickly joined him around the spreadout newspaper. At the top of the front page was the title, *The Miami Herald,* and Jenny instantly forgot the newscast when she recognized a photo halfway down the page. It was one of Uncle Pete, probably dug out of some old company file.

Justin read aloud, "The United States government is presenting strong protests to the Colombian guerrillas over the kidnapping of a prominent American citizen. FARC, the largest guerrilla group, presently negotiating with the Colombian government to become a recognized political party, has denied all involvement in the kidnapping . . ."

Looking over his shoulder, Estrella interrupted sarcastically, "Your government is always using its power to lean on those less fortunate. What right do they have to make demands here?"

"Don't you think they have a right to protest when someone kidnaps one of their citizens?" Justin answered in surprise.

"And don't say *your* government," Jenny added hotly. "If you have an American father, then you are an American citizen too!"

Estrella clenched her fists. "Don't you call me that. I want nothing of my father's! I will never be American!"

Brown and blue sparks clashed as the two girls stared at each other. Justin said mildly, "Lay off, Jenny! She's just repeating what someone told her!"

As the two girls lowered their angry eyes, he dropped into an armchair and said, "Estrella, you never did tell us about your father. Do you still remember him? Who was he? Why did he go away?"

Sitting down on the sofa, Estrella answered slowly, "Yes, I remember him. He . . . he was a big man with eyes as blue as mine. I . . . I used to run to meet him when he came home each night. He would throw me up to the ceiling and laugh. My mother would laugh, too. That is what I remember best— the laughing, the happiness! His name was . . . yes, I do remember . . . it was Gary Adams."

She pronounced the name with an odd foreign accent. "But I did not call him that. He taught me the American word . . . 'Daddy.' He always spoke to me in English and was proud that I learned his language better than my mother. He went away often, but my mother always told me he had gone to his country on business and that he would be back. And he always did come back. Until one day. . ."

Estrella stared blindly at the blank wall opposite her, her eyes focused on long-ago memories. "I remember . . . I was going to be eight years old. He hugged me when he left. He told me he loved me . . . that he would be back soon . . . that he would bring me a present for my birthday!"

Estrella sat stiffly on the edge of the sofa, tears trickling down her face. Jenny moved over and put a sympethetic arm around her as she continued, almost in a whisper. "He never came back! He never even sent a letter! We waited and waited!

"My mother spent the money he had left. Then she got sick. If only I could have brought a doctor . . . but there was no money even for medicine. It was his fault she died! And then they said I had to leave. I could pay no rent."

She shrugged Jenny's arm away angrily. "I was on the street for months! Do you know what it is like to live on the streets? To have no one who cares if you live or die?"

Justin tried to imagine life without Mom, who would always drop what she was doing when he dashed in from school to ask in her gentle voice about his day. Or without Dad, squealing into the driveway every night in the old station wagon with some crazy new idea for a family outing. He had a sudden mental picture of a forlorn little boy huddled in a drafty cardboard box. He said slowly, "Yeah, we've seen it. It's awful!"

"I'll never forgive him!" Estrella said fiercely, wiping at her cheeks with the back of her hand. "I'll never forgive my father for what he did to my mother . . . and to me!"

There was an uncomfortable silence. As Estrella stared down at her clenched fists, Justin suddenly remembered something his Sunday school teacher had said the Sunday before they left Seattle. "I'm really sorry about your father, Estrella. It's been terrible for you."

He added hesitantly, "But you can't keep hating your father for the rest of your life! God says to forgive other people just like He forgave all the bad things *we've* done."

"God!" Estrella replied scornfully as she jumped off the couch. "You two sound just like Doña Rosa! Always talking about God and telling me to forgive my father!"

"Doña Rosa?" the twins chorused together, trying to pronounce the name as Estrella had: Do-nee-a Ro-sa. "Who's she?" asked Justin.

Then Jenny demanded, "I thought you said you didn't have any friends . . . just your 'family'! Who's this Doña Rosa?"

"Doña Rosa is. . ." Estrella sat down again, looking shamefaced. "Well, you know how I told you about Carlos finding me on the street?"

They nodded, and she went on. "That was true, but not all the truth. One day soon after Carlos found me, I was at the . . . What do you call it?—the garbage heap. I was looking for something to eat. This lady . . . she had brought her garbage. . . I knew her and she knew me. She had once lived in our neighborhood—she sewed clothes for me and my mother.

"She was so sorry to see me there. She took me to her home. Her husband was kind to me, too. I was there many weeks. They talked like you . . . like those words you said in Zipaquirá. I can't remember them all."

Looking at each other, Justin and Jenny repeated, "And be ye kind one to another, tender-hearted, forgiving one another, even s God for Christ's sake hath forgiven you."

"Yes, Doña Rosa was like that . . . kind and compassionate. She kept telling me I must forgive my father and forget what he had done . . . that I would never be happy until I forgave him."

Her expression softened suddenly. "I wonder sometimes what happened to Doña Rosa. She cried when Carlos took me away. She and her husband had no children of their own. They wanted me to stay forever!"

"Why did you leave, then?" Jenny asked, confused. "It sounds like they were nice people!"

"I didn't like her words," Estrella admitted. "I was very angry. Then Carlos found me. The people on the street told him where I had gone. He told me that God was a lie—that Doña Rosa and her husband were foolish.

"One day Doña Rosa had to move . . . her husband had a new job. They wanted me to go with them, but Carlos came and told me that he had a place for me . . . that with him I could fight against people who would leave children to starve in the street."

Estella waved an expressive hand. "So I went with him . . . and that is all!"

Jenny sniffed. "Well, it seems to me it would have been smarter to stay with this Doña Rosa."

"Yeah, Doña Rosa was right—about forgiving your father, I mean," Justin added.

Estrella jumped up again. "It is easy for you to say this!" she stormed angrily. "If you were me, you would not forgive either!"

She turned and ran from the lounge, leaving the twins looking blankly at each other. After a long moment, Justin shrugged and said, "Well, I guess she really has had it pretty rough!"

"Yeah, I don't know *what* I'd do if Dad just disappeared someday." Jenny frowned. "No wonder she doesn't trust Americans."

Estrella didn't reappear that evening, but Steve showed up briefly before they went to bed. As he read through his usual stack of reports, Justin asked him, "Steve, how would you find someone who's missing?"

When Steve looked up in surprise, Justin explained, "It's Estrella's dad. Do you think you could find out what happened to him?"

"Well, if you know his name, and when he was last in Bogota, I suppose we could do some checking," Steve answered thoughtfully. He looked suddenly interested. "What did you say his name was?"

Steve promised to look through the embassy passport records for any information about a Gary Adams. Estrella was in bed when the twins went upstairs and was nowhere to be found when they got up the next morning. She didn't appear for breakfast, but neither Steve nor Mr. Bascom were there, and the security guard who dished up scrambled eggs and bacon only made a comment about kids sleeping in while soldiers! had to slave for their country.

When Estrella still hadn't appeared by eleven o'clock,

Justin began to feel uneasy. She had never been gone this long, and Justin knew Steve or Mr. Bascom would be certain to ask where she was if she didn't show up soon. As though his thoughts had summoned them, Steve and Mr. Bascom chose that moment to walk into the lounge together.

He stopped short as he caught sight of the twins. "Don't worry, kids! We're sure to find your uncle any time. We're doing all we can!"

But he didn't sound at all convincing, and the twins exchanged a worried look. Jenny made a slight motion with her head, and Justin followed her out of the lounge and back upstairs. Shutting the door to her room behind them, Jenny said with determination, "Justin, don't you think it's strange that every tip Estrella has given Steve has come up a dead end?"

Justin sat down on the bed. "No, I don't! You know Estrella told us people wouldn't talk to Steve."

"Well, Estrella hasn't come up with anything either, has she!" Jenny answered. "I'm beginning to wonder if she's really trying."

Justin walked over to the barred window and stared down at the dusty alley. "Come off it, Jenny! I'm worried about Uncle Pete too. But you can't blame Estrella!"

"I'm not blaming her!" Jenny slid off the bed and joined him at the window. "I'm just asking questions that need answers. Like why, if Estrella has hated Americans for so many years, did she suddenly decide to talk to us at that museum?"

Reading Justin's thoughts before he could answer, she added, "Yes, I know she was sorry for being so rude and wanted to be our friend. But why did she come over to talk to us in the first place? She must have known we were Americans the minute we opened our mouths!

"And there at Simon Bolivar's house! It just seems too

much of a coincidence that those guerrillas showed up right after Estrella called us out."

"Jenny, she saved our lives!" Justin answered impatiently. "Why would she do that if she wasn't doing her best to help us?"

"Oh, come on, Justin! That bomb didn't come anywhere near us, and you know it!" Jenny answered scornfully. She looked suddenly exasperated. "What's got into you, Justin? Usually, you'd be the one asking questions—*and* wondering what Estrella's up to!"

Justin shook his head stubbornly. "This is different. I *know* Estrella was telling the truth when she said she wanted to be our friend. I can tell she really cares about us!"

Before Jenny could argue further, the door slammed open. Both Justin and Jenny were startled into silence as Estrella burst into the room, her pale features ablaze with excitement. Justin cast a glance of triumph at his sister as Estrella annnounced, "I've found him! At last I have found your uncle!"

Chapter 8

Betrayed!

"Estrella, that's great! Where is he? Is he okay? How did you find out?" Justin and Jenny's questions tumbled over each other. Jenny—her suspicions swept away—was as excited as Justin.

Justin started for the door. "Well, come on you two! We've got to find Steve right away! Once Estrella tells him where Uncle Pete is, Steve can take his men in there to get him out in no time!"

"Just one moment!" Estrella blocked the doorway. "You do not understand. I cannot tell Steve where your uncle is. I do not even know!"

Bewildered, Justin demanded, "But, Estrella, you said you found him!"

"I have learned where he is, but I don't know exactly how to get there," Estrella explained. She added quickly, "But that does not matter. I have a friend who does know. He will help us find your uncle."

Sitting on the edge of Jenny's bed, she told them how an

acquaintance had admitted that he had heard rumors of an American hostage. "I told him that your uncle was a friend of mine, and begged him to tell me what he knew. He was frightened and would tell me nothing at first, but at last he told me that he knew the man who takes supplies to the group that holds your uncle. From this man he learned where your uncle is being held."

"Then your friend will help Steve and the soldiers rescue Uncle Pete!" Justin said with satisfaction.

"No!" Surprised at her violent response, the twins stared at Estrella. The young guerrilla girl jumped to her feet. "No! Have you forgotten who I am? Never will I deliver freedom fighters into the hands of the soldiers—not even for you! Nor would my friend ever lead soldiers to the camp."

The excitement drained from Justin and Jenny's faces. Jenny demanded angrily, "Why did you bother finding him if you aren't going to tell us where he is? You promised to help us rescue him!"

"But of course I will help you!" Estrella said with a shrug of her slim shoulders. "It is very simple. I will take you to your uncle—and no one else!"

The twins stared at Estrella skeptically. Justin found his voice first. "Are you crazy, Estrella? You don't really think three kids can walk into a guerrilla hideout and just grab Uncle Pete, do you?"

Estrella looked very pleased with herself. "I told you this man I know will help. He has everything planned, and he will be armed. There are no more than two guards where your uncle is. It will not be difficult."

"Well, that's great, Estrella!" Justin said, a little doubtfully. "You've certainly been a great friend!"

Estrella stared at Justin, a strange expression flickering in the black-fringed, blue eyes. She looked away. Turning toward the door, she said in a hard voice, "Well, are you coming with me or not?"

This time it was Jenny who blocked the doorway. "Just a minute! Justin was right. This is crazy! You haven't even told us where we're going! Is Uncle Pete still in Bogota? How long will we be gone? What do we need to take with us?"

Planting her feet firmly, she crossed her arms. "I'm not moving from here till I get a few answers!"

Seeing Jenny's determined expression, Justin added his support. "Come on, Estrella! We're your friends! You can at least tell us where we're going!"

Estrella looked sulky, but at last shrugged her shoulders. "I guess it does not really matter. You will find out soon enough!"

She pointed at Jenny's jacket, lying in a heap at the foot of her bed. "We are going into the mountains, so you will need that. It is not far—an hour or two past Armero. We will have your uncle back here before dark."

Justin nodded agreement, but Jenny shook her head with a frown. "I don't know. I think we should at least leave a message for Steve—let him know where we're going. What if something goes wrong? He won't have any idea where we are!"

Estrella's pale cheeks were stained red with anger. "No! If you tell Steve anything, I will leave and so will my friend. You will never see your uncle again!"

Justin looked at his sister, his jaw set with determination. "Jenny, we have to go! If we hadn't talked Uncle Pete into going with us that afternoon, he wouldn't be in this fix. You know Steve said they might never find him. If there's even a chance we can get him back, we've got to try!"

There was a long moment of silence, then Jenny nodded. "Yeah, I guess you're right! We don't really have much choice."

"Then let us go!" Estrella said urgently. "We have already wasted much time!"

"Just a minute! I'll get my jacket." Justin dashed next door and picked up his jacket from the chair where he had tossed it. He was pulling it on when he paused. *Jenny's right,* he thought suddenly. *No matter what Estrella says, we can't just run off without telling anyone. Steve would think we'd been kidnapped too.*

Grabbing the newspaper he had brought up the day before, he tore a strip from the broad margin that eged the paper. Pulling out a pencil, he scribbled rapidly, "Steve, Estrella's taking us to Uncle Pete. The mountains—an hour or two past Armero. Don't worry about us. We should have Uncle Pete back by tonight."

He was looking for a place to put the note when he had a sudden thought. Unfolding it, he hastily added a rough sketch of the turtle-shaped car he had seen at Zipaquirá. Folding the note into a tiny rectangle as he hurried into the connecting bathroom, he stuffed it into the frame of the mirror over the sink.

He had just returned to the other room and was pulling on his jacket when Estrella pushed open the door. She looked around the room so suspiciously that Justin was glad he hadn't left the note on the table as he had at first planned. She asked impatiently, "What is taking so long?"

"Just had to use the bathroom! I'm ready to go now," Justin answered hastily, zipping up his jacket and following her into the hall.

The three children walked casually down the wide stairs.

There was no one in sight. Estrella led them down a dark passageway toward the back of the house and into an unlocked room piled high with cardboard boxes and barrels.

Half-used buckets of paint stood in one corner, and remnants of rope and other odds-and-ends hung on the walls. Justin grinned to himself as Estrella paused behind a tall stack of boxes to pry out the screen that covered an air vent. So *this* was how Estrella had been getting out of the house!

The tunnel behind the vent screen was too small to permit the passage of an adult. Estrella and Jenny wormed their way through with ease, but Justin had to force his wider shoulders through the narrow space. He was breathing hard by the time he tumbled out behind the girls into a small, dark room. From the clink of cutlery and the odors filtering through the cracks in a wooden door, Justin guessed they were in one of the kitchen storerooms.

Crouching behind a pair of large, galvanized metal cans that—judging by the smell!—held a month's supply of the guest house kitchen's garbage, Estrella pointed toward a faint red light that indicated one of the surveillance cameras high on the ceiling in the opposite corner of the small room. Then she motioned toward a dark, square opening in the floor, sheltered from the view of the moving camera by the garbage cans.

Estrella disappeared feet first into the opening, and Jenny reluctantly followed her. Then Justin swung his feet into the opening and found himself sliding quickly down some sort of metal chute—obviously meant for the kitchen garbage. His shoulders jammed as the chute leveled out at the bottom, and he felt a momentary panic until the two girls tugged him free.

Justin carefully climbed off the pile of black plastic bags of garbage that lay at the foot of the chute. He was standing in a dusty alley that ran along the back of the guest house. The sun was shining, but a cold breeze whistled down the alley, and Justin pulled his jacket close.

"Wow!" he said with admiration as he peered back up the dark garbage chute. "Estrella, how did you learn about this?"

She shrugged. "Buildings are much alike. There are few from which one cannot escape."

She seemed nervous as she urged the twins quickly down the alley. Justin too looked back frequently as Estrella led them through several small side streets, but no one seemed to have discovered their escape. About three blocks from the guest house, Justin suddenly caught sight of a familiar red Volkswagen *peta*. Lounging against the side of the car was the young driver he had seen at the Salt Cathedral.

"Hey, I've seen that guy before! He's your friend, isn't he?" Justin exclaimed.

Estrella abruptly stopped and demanded, "How would you know about him?"

"I saw him with you at the Salt Cathedral," Justin explained. "I had a feeling he might be the man you were talking about!"

Estrella looked displeased, but she admitted as they reached the red car, "Yes, this is Alejandro. He will take us to your uncle."

She added something in Spanish, and the young man, who looked only half-a-dozen years older than Justin, straightened up. Pulling off a pair of sunglasses, he stared down at Justin and Jenny, his dark features cold and unfriendly. Then he growled something to Estrella and opened the back door of the car.

Pushing the twins toward the open door, Estrella said impatiently, "Come on! He says we must hurry!"

Justin instinctively disliked the young man. Reluctantly, he followed Jenny into the back seat. Estrella climbed into the front seat beside the driver. Ignoring the twins completely, the young man she had called Alejandro slammed on the accelerator, barely missing an oncoming truck as he zoomed onto a main avenue.

Though fast, the young man was not a good driver. He pushed in and out of the heavy traffic with complete disregard of traffic laws. In the front seat, Estrella and the driver were speaking quietly together in Spanish. Justin leaned over to whisper to his sister, "I don't trust this guy! I hope Estrella knows what she's doing!"

Her knuckles white as the car swerved to miss by inches what seemed a certain collision with a bus, Jenny whispered back, "You were the one who wanted to come!"

Justin had no answer to that. He watched alertly as they left the city behind, and quickly recognized this as the highway Steve had taken to the Salt Cathedral. But they soon turned onto a two-lane paved road that headed directly toward the great mountain range that surrounded the valley of Bogota.

No one spoke as Alejandro slowed through several small towns with whitewashed buildings. There was little traffic. But occasionally Justin heard the drone of an airplane. And once, he glimpsed a helicopter lazily tracing patterns overhead.

He leaned forward suddenly as he caught sight of a familiar-looking snowcapped peak ahead, its heavy, graywhite plum drifting up to lose itself in the bank of clouds that was closing in over the mountains.

"Hey, Jenny, there's that mountain again—the Nevada del Ruiz! Look at all that smoke! Maybe it's about to erupt!"

"It always looks like that," Estrella answered from the front seat in a bored voice.

Justin was about to tell her what they had seen on the news when, with no slackening of speed, Alejandro turned onto a dirt road that wound up into the foothills of the mountain range. All three children clung to their seats as the dirt road grew narrower and bumpier. The cloud cover seemed to drop to the ground, and fog soon blotted out all but the road directly ahead.

The red Volkswagen hit an extra-large bump that crashed Justin and Jenny against the roof of the car, then Alejandro slammed to a stop. Climbing out, he hurried around to the back of the car. Opening the passenger door, Estrella pulled the seat forward and motioned impatiently to the twins. "Come on! We have to walk from here."

They climbed out. The fog pressed in around them, but Justin could see that the dirt road had ended on a ridge of the mountains. They were above the tree-line here, but in the gullies sweeping downward on either side were stunted cypress, tamarack, and junipers.

A strong, icy wind blew through their jackets. Justin took in a deep breath that stung his lungs with cold, then sniffed at the air again. "What's that smell?" he demanded. "It smells like rotten eggs!"

Estrella looked impatient. "I don't smell anything! Come! We have no time to waste."

Alejandro had opened a door of the little car and yanked out a backpack. He lifted the pack to his back, then pulled out a machine gun of the same type the soldiers had carried in the airport.

Jenny gasped as the young man checked the gun for bullets and slung an extra belt of bullets over one shoulder. "What does he need that for?"

"Yeah, we wouldn't want to shoot anyone!" Justin said with determination.

"And how did you think we would get your uncle out?" Estrella replied scornfully. "Do you think you can just say 'please' to the guards, and they will let your uncle go?"

She added smoothly, "Of course we will not hurt anyone. If the guards see that Alejandro is armed, they will let your uncle go without any shooting."

Alejandro slammed the car door shut, and his sharp words whirled the children around. Estrella translated his order. "We are leaving the car here. We must go that way."

The three children followed Alejandro up the bank where the road ended and along the top of the mountain ridge. There was no path, but they picked their way across the springy, moss-like grass that cloaked the mountain meadow with green. Justin's tennis shoes were soon soaked through and he could see that Jenny was shivering. Though she wore only a thin windbreaker, Estrella seemed immune to the cold.

Alejandro came to a halt at the edge of a gully. With his machine gun, he pointed out a faint animal trail that led down into a tangle of evergreens. The same wind that bit through their clothing had carved these evergreens into short, twisted forms not much taller than a man.

No one else seemed to notice the odd smell that still caught at the back of Justin's nostrils, and he wondered if he could be imagining it. As the two girls scrambled down the trail ahead of him, he paused to wipe his fog-wet face with a jacket sleeve. He looked with keen interest at the gray-white streak left on his sleeve.

A sudden blow to his back pushed him down the trail. Justin looked up angrily. Alejandro, his dark eyes cold and watchful, pointed his machine gun impatiently down into the gully. Estrella, already at the bottom, called up to him, "Justin, come! We have not much time!"

Justin scrambled down hastily to join his sister and Estrella. As they threaded their way through the evergreen thickets, Justin glanced back at Alejandro, his machine gun cradled easily across his arms as he brought up the rear.

Pushing a soggy branch out of his face, Justin muttered loudly, "I thought he was supposed to be leading us, not taking us prisoner!"

Estrella, at the front of the single-file line, looked back. "He is making sure no one follows us."

Justin was suddenly reminded of the note he had tucked into the bathroom mirror. He wondered if Steve had found it.

The fog had rolled away by the time Alejandro finally brought them to a stop. They had been climbing up and down one gully after another for more than an hour, scrambling over logs, wading across shallow streams, and occasionally breaking into the welcome short grass of a mountain meadow.

Now they were on flat ground—a small mountain plateau choked with underbrush. Here the evergreens grew tall, in the shelter of the mountain ridges that pressed close overhead. The trail they now followed bore the obvious marks of human feet, but they could see only a few feet ahead, and Justin had lost all sense of direction.

Alejandro pushed them into the partial shelter of a tangled thicket, and the twins squatted down to rest while Estrella and Alejandro held a whispered conference. The growling of his stomach reminded Justin that they had missed lunch.

Estrella walked over and squatted down beside them. "The camp is just ahead—down in a canyon. Alejandro and I will check out the camp—to make sure there have been no changes since our last information. You two will stay here out of sight."

Justin protested. "Why should we stay here? Wouldn't it be safer if we all stuck together?'

"You do not know how to move silently as we do," Estrella answered flatly. "You would bring danger to us. If you stay here out of sight, you will be safe enough. We will be back in just a few minutes. If there are still just two guards, we will take you in to get your uncle."

Estrella jumped to her feet as Alejandro snapped out a Spanish order. At the sight of his scowling face and expertly held machine gun, Justin didn't argue. Alejandro and Estrella disappeared without a sound into the underbrush, and Justin admitted to himself that he could never move that quietly.

The twins huddled further into the thicket. The tangled branches of a pair of junipers trailed to the ground around them. Here, the weak rays of a late-afternoon sun couldn't reach their damp clothing, and without the exercise of walking to warm them, both children were soon shivering.

Justin glanced over at his sister. Her dark curls were plastered to her head, and her lips were blue with cold. She frowned. "I hope they come back soon! At this rate we'll never get back before dark!"

In fact, no more than five minutes had passed when they heard a twig crack on the path just outside the thicket. Justin whispered eagerly to his sister, "There they are! Let's go."

But it was neither Estrella nor Alejandro who poked a head into the thicket where they crouched. Justin's mouth fell open as Steve Cardoza squatted down on his haunches and, holding a branch out of his face, said softly, "Hello, kids!"

"Steve! How did you find us so fast?" Justin exclaimed. The enormous relief he felt made him realize how much he had counted on Steve finding his note. Now everything would be all right!

As Steve dropped the branch behind him and joined them in the thicket, Jenny demanded, "How did you find us at all? Estrella's going to be really mad when she sees you here!"

Justin sheepishly told his sister of the note he had left behind. "I was afraid you wouldn't see it!" he told Steve.

"You couldn't have been gone long when I came up to look for you," Steve explained quickly in a low voice. "I searched your rooms up and down once the security guards confirmed you weren't in the building."

He looked approvingly at Justin. "That sketch of the car—that was good thinking. I remembered what you'd told me about Estrella's acquaintance in the red car, and got on the phone right away to a friend over at the Colombian Air Force. I asked him to call out a couple of helicopters to check out every mountain road leading out past Armero for a red Volkswagen *peta.*"

Justin suddenly remembered the helicopter he had seen tracing patterns overhead—what seemed like hours ago. Steve went on, "Of course, I knew there was a good chance you might have taken a different vehicle, but it was the only lead we had. And it paid off!"

He grinned. "I was already at Armero when the helicopter radioed that they'd seen your car heading up this way. I found the *peta* abandoned at the end of the road and followed your tracks. None of you took much care to cover them. I'm sure glad to find you here safe and sound."

His grin suddenly disappeared as he leaned forward. In a stern whisper, he demanded, "Now tell me what ever possessed you to go off like this! This is the most stupid stunt I've ever seen! Don't you know better than to let that little guerrilla friend of yours talk you into something like *this?*

You could have been killed!"

Both children squirmed under his sharp words, but Justin defended Estrella. "Estrella didn't want anyone to get hurt. She said you'd bring in soldiers and maybe get some of the guerrillas killed—and Uncle Pete, too! She and her friend have it all planned. There are only two guards, and Alejandro can take care of them. They'll be back in just a few minutes, and we can get Uncle Pete out without any shooting!"

Steve shook his head grimly. "It was still stupid! Anyway, we'd better try to get your uncle and get out of here. This is a very dangerous place to be right now."

"What do you mean?" Justin asked curiously.

"I mean that we're too close to the Nevada del Ruiz. Don't you remember they announced yesterday that they were expecting another blowup?"

"But you said it would just be a little one—that the mud and snow would just go down the mountain canyons!" Jenny protested. Her voice trailed off as she caught her breath.

"That smell! It was *sulfur!*" Justin exclaimed suddenly. He brushed at the faint powdering of gray-white dust that coated his jacket. "This dust must be ash falling!"

"That's right," Steve added grimly. "And that melt-off will be heading this way. These guerrillas obviously don't pay close enough attention to the news."

He turned to leave the thicket. "By the way, Justin, it's unlikely that you'd find only two guards in a guerrilla camp. Which way did you say Estrella and her friend went?"

Crawling out of the thicket behind him, Justin pointed out the direction. In spite of the tongue-lashing, he had to admit that the presence of the tough Marine lieutenant was enough to send his optimism soaring.

Steve said calmly, "I'll take a look. You two stay here and

don't move!"

"Oh, please, can't we go along?" Justin protested. "We'll be quiet!"

Steve nodded curtly, his keen eyes expertly scanning for any movement. "Okay! But you step where I step and do what I do—and don't make a sound!"

Jenny, holding a branch back to look out of the thicket, made no move to follow them. When Justin looked back at her in surprise, she said, "I'll wait for Estrella. Someone has to tell her where you are."

They had only moved a few dozen yards through the thick undergrowth, Justin following Steve's footsteps as quietly as he could, when they heard faint voices. Dropping to his stomach, Steve hissed, "Get down!"

He wriggled forward through a tangle of brush, then stopped. Wriggling up beside him, Justin's heart skipped a beat as he saw what had frozen the Marine Lieutenant to this spot.

About thirty feet below them was a wide gully—almost a narrow valley—pierced through the center by a rapidly-moving stream. Two crude thatched huts perched on the bank of the creek and, directly below the brush thicket where Steve and Justin crouched, several small Army-style tents formed a circle with the huts and the canyon wall. At least half-a-dozen men huddled around a bonfire in the center.

That's a lot more than two guards! Justin thought angrily. *I never did trust that Alejandro! I hope he didn't lead Estrella into a trap!* But it wasn't Alejandro who walked that moment into the smoky light of the fire, laughing and clinging to the arm of a tall, slim man with a commanding stride who carried a machine gun slung over the other shoulder.

"It can't be Estrella!" Justin whispered blankly. "But . . . but it is!"

Chapter 9

The Guerrilla Camp

Justin stared in horror at the scene below, trying to persuade himself that Estrella was a prisoner. But just then, the tall commander bent his head to speak to Estrella and her tinkling laugh rang out in response. He shook his head numbly and whispered, "I don't understand! She's our friend! What's she doing down there?"

Steve reached over and grabbed Justin by the wrist. "Don't you get it? That's Estrella's guerrilla band down there—her 'family'! She led you into a trap!"

Turning his head to catch Steve's grim expression, Justin made a discovery. "You aren't surprised! Did you know?"

"I never did trust that girl!" Steve answered bluntly. "I've been checking around her old neighborhood. This morning one of the neighbors told me they'd heard a couple of men from here were arrested. I was on my way to ask Estrella about it when I found you gone."

Steve began to slither backward. "Your uncle is probably in one of the tents—or one of those huts. Let's go get Jenny.

We'll have to go for help and hope they don't move your uncle before we get some soldiers up here."

Justin watched the scene below a moment longer. He shook his head in amazement as Estrella laughingly greeted the other men around the fire. She had seemed so sincere. He could have sworn she desperately wanted their friendship. There had to be an explanation!

"Justin!" At Steve's urgent command, Justin began to wriggle quietly backward. He was out of the brush and about to stand up when he heard a sudden thud and a grunt of pain.

"Steve?" he called quietly.

There was a rustle in the tangled brush beside him. Justin froze as he heard heavy footsteps, then slowly turned his head. He stared at the combat boots planted firmly inches from his nose. They were dusty and scuffed, and very, very real. His eyes rose slowly upward to focus on a rifle held in rock-steady hands.

Justin slowly rolled over and sat up, raising his arms in the air. The rifle didn't waver, and his gaze moved upward to meet a pair of young, black eyes that burned with hatred. He turned his head cautiously. Steve lay on the ground a few feet away, blood streaming down one side of his face from a cut on his head. Standing over him was an older guerrilla, an M-16 machine gun cradled in one arm.

Steve groaned, then slowly sat up. As soon as the two guerrillas saw that he had regained consciousness, they motioned for their two captives to stand up. Aware of the rifle only inches from his stomach, Justin jumped to his feet, carefully keeping his hands in the air.

Shaking the blood from his eyes, Steve didn't move fast enough for their two captors, and the older guerrilla jabbed him in the stomach with the butt of his machine gun. Wiping a hand across his face, Steve swayed to his feet.

Just then Justin heard his sister's angry voice. "Let go, Alejandro! You're hurting my arm!"

A moment later, Alejandro—smiling for the first time since they'd met him—shoved Jenny into their midst. Catching sight of her brother, Jenny exclaimed breathlessly, "Justin, I don't know what's got into Alejandro! Have you seen Estrella?"

Her voice trailed off in a gasp as she caught sight of the two armed guerrillas. "You mean . . . Alejandro's one of them? One of the guerrillas?"

She looked around as the two guerrillas, their guns trained on their three captives, spoke in Spanish with Alejandro. "I suppose they got Estrella, too!" Jenny continued.

Justin shook his head wearily and motioned toward the gully. Estrella was now seated on the edge of a roughly-built picnic table beside the fire. Jenny stiffened as Estrella's voice suddenly rang out in a laugh. Sadly she declared, "I knew it! I never did trust her."

Alejandro suddenly barked out an order, and Justin's captor used his rifle butt to push him toward the edge of the cliff. Stepping around the bushes, Justin caught sight of a very steep trail that cut diagonally across the cliff face, down into the gully.

As he started down the path, he saw that the gully widened into an open valley downstream. But about half a mile upstream, it narrowed into a bottleneck canyon that wound up into the hills. Half-slipping down the steep trail wide enough only for one slim person, he caught a faint glimpse of snowy peaks upstream, stained with the red of sunset.

Two women were clearing a pile of dirty metal plates from the picnic table when their captors shoved Steve and the twins into the circle of tattered tents and huts. Everyone in the camp paused to watch their approach, and Estrella hopped down from the table, waving a slim arm.

"Justin! Jenny! You're all right, aren't you?"

She motioned toward the slim, dark man who leaned unmoving against the picnic table. "I told you that you would meet Carlos one day."

Her welcoming smile turned to a scowl as she noticed Steve. "What is *he* doing here?'

The man she had called Carlos didn't even look at the children as he barked out an order, and the two guerrillas who had captured Justin and Steve shoved the Marine lieutenant toward one of the huts. Carlos followed them, leaving Justin and Jenny standing alone with Estrella. Justin quickly scanned the camp, but any thoughts of dashing into the darkness evaporated at the sight of Alejandro lounging against a nearby tree, machine gun cradled and ready.

Confusion fought with anger as Justin turned to the young guerrilla girl and demanded roughly, "Estrella, what's going on? Where's Uncle Pete?"

A shrill bark rang out. A little dog with tangled, dusty-white hair dashed out from behind a tent, and suddenly everything became horribly clear to Justin. "You were the girl with the dog—the one who sent that message to Uncle Pete! You've been in this all along!"

As Estrella leaned down to pick up the dog, Jenny added scornfully, "Yeah, it was no 'accident' when you met us at the Gold Museum, was it? I'll bet you'd been following us the whole time! You were the one who led the guerrillas to capture Uncle Pete. And you pretended to feel so sorry for us!"

Estrella flushed with embarrassment as Jenny looked her

up and down with disgust, and Jenny added impatiently, "What I don't understand is, why this silly play-acting? Why didn't you just take us all at once?"

For the first time since her greeting, Estrella spoke up. "They did not want you—only your uncle. But he will not cooperate. Carlos told me to bring you here so that your uncle will do as he is told."

She lifted her chin defiantly. "You don't understand! Your uncle's people took our friends—Eduardo and Paco. Now they are in prison. It is only fair that we should take your uncle. With his help, we can get them out."

"There is a difference!" Justin answered shortly. "Those men were criminals. Mr. Bascom said two men were killed when they tried to bomb the pipeline. The police had every right to put them in jail."

Estrella's eyes flashed. "No! That is not true. They wouldn't kill anyone! Nor will anyone hurt you. All we want is to get Eduardo and Paco out of jail."

Her expression was half-pleading, half-defiant. "Don't you understand? They are my 'family.' I *had* to help get them out!"

Justin said bitterly, "So you pretended to be our friend. And all the time it was just another of Carlos' orders. I suppose all that time you were out 'looking for Uncle Pete,' you were just going out to get orders from Carlos. How could I have been so stupid!"

Justin didn't often lose his temper, but when he did, all his friends knew to get out of his way. The hot anger and hurt that had been building up since he had first seen Estrella in the guerrilla camp tightened into a hard lump in his chest.

Clenching his fists, he exploded, "You are a liar and a cheat, Estrella! We were your friends! We cared about you.

And you were pretending and lying to us all the time!"

"But I am your friend! I would not hurt you!" Estrella stepped forward just as Alejandro moved to separate the three angry children.

As the young guerrilla shoved the twins toward one of the tents, Justin glared back at Estrella. "I'll never forgive you for this, Estrella! Never!"

The tent Alejandro took them to lay back under a cluster of tamaracks. A guard stood at attention in front. As Alejandro raised the tent flap and shoved the two children inside, Justin and Jenny caught sight of a bound and gagged figure half-sitting, half-lying at the far side of the tent.

"Uncle Pete!" Jenny cried joyfully, almost knocking him over with her exuberant bear hug. "You really *are* here!"

"At least she told the truth about something!" Justin muttered as he quickly knelt behind his uncle. "Come on, Jenny! Help me get him untied."

Jenny yanked off the dirty strip of cloth that had served as a gag, while Justin struggled with the tight knots that bound Uncle Pete's hands behind his back. Uncle Pete didn't look at all pleased to see his niece and nephew. The instant the gag was off, he said gloomily, "So they got you too. I overheard their planning, but I hoped you wouldn't fall for it."

Justin finally loosened the last knot. As the rope fell to the ground, Uncle Pete rubbed his swollen wrists and looked sternly at his niece and nephew. "How could you fall for that girl's story? Didn't you have more sense than to try to rescue me single-handed?"

Both twins looked shamefaced, and Uncle Pete sighed. "Well, it's done now. Okay, tell me what happened."

They had only a few minutes to recount the happenings of the last few days when the tent flap lifted again and a guerrilla motioned to the three to step outside. He too carried a machine gun—obviously the favorite weapon of the guerrillas—and waved it toward the three Parkers as he led them back to the fire.

It was pitch dark now, and the only light was that of the campfire. The whole group of guerrillas had gathered, and Justin counted eight men and three women. All were dressed in mismatched bits of civilian clothing and Colombian army uniforms.

Steve also was there, a rough bandage now covering the gash on the side of his head. His battered face was expressionless, but his eyes were alert. *He'll do something to get us out of here,* Justin thought hopefully. But Steve's hands were tied tightly behind him, and one guard kept a gun trained on his back.

A brisk wind whistled down the canyon, and Justin was suddenly aware of how cold he was in his still-damp clothing. A branch snapped in the fire, and the flames flared up, casting red shadows across the angry face of the tall leader of the guerrilla band.

"Señor Parker, you have been very uncooperative!" he snapped in strongly accented English. "Our comrades have not been released."

Still clutching her dog, Estrella sat on the edge of the picnic table, intently watching as the guerrilla leader waved a threatening arm. "Now we have your family and this American spy. Surely your government will consider the four of you an adequate exchange for release of our comrades."

Uncle Pete looked regretfully down at his niece and nephew, but he shook his head firmly. "Carlos, I have explained this to you before. There is nothing I can do to secure the release of your men. Neither your government nor ours will give in to your demands. Extra hostages won't make any difference at all!"

Estrella was suddenly at Justin's side. She whispered urgently, "You must convince him to let our friends go! Please!"

Carlos looked furious. "Do you think I am a fool? You are an important man, Señor Parker. Your embassy will do what you command. You and your family will not leave here until our demands are met."

Steve took a sudden step forward. "We can't stay here! Like I told you already, we've *all* got to get out of here—and soon!"

He nodded toward the surrounding mountain peaks, now masked by darkness. "The Nevada del Ruiz is due to erupt again soon, and this place will be right in the path. Have you forgotten Armero?"

The events of the last hour had driven the strange odor in the air out of Justin's mind, but he suddenly realized the smell of sulfur had grown stronger. Carlos' sharp features showed uncertainty, then his expression hardened. "I have already told you that this is nonsense. If this were so, we would have heard about it."

"Only a small eruption is expected. If you'd been listening to the news you would have heard about it. It won't reach any towns, and there aren't supposed to be any people in this area. But you're right in the canyon! You should at least move up to high ground."

Steve looked around impatiently at the rest of the small band. "Haven't you seen the smoke rising from the mountain?"

The rest of the guerrillas stared back blankly, unable to understand Steve's words, but Carlos answered curtly, "There is always smoke above the Nevada del Ruiz."

"But is there always ash falling? Look for yourselves!" Steve walked over to a tree and rubbed his jacket sleeve on the trunk. The thin film of gray-white ash was clearly seen against the dark-brown leather.

The guerrilla leader ran a finger down his own sleeve, then spit on the ground. "It is nothing but dust blown by the wind—the same dust we have seen since we camped here."

Before Steve could say anything else, he added sharply, "This is but a trick to escape from here, but it will not work! We will wait no longer. Your embassy will be informed tonight of your capture. They have until morning to announce the release of our comrades. If it doesn't happen, . . . then you will all be very sorry you ever came to this country!"

Carlos snapped an order, and Alejandro and another guerrilla herded the captives back toward the tent. While the other guerrilla stood guard, Alejandro roughly bound their hands and feet. As they left the tent, Justin slumped against the tent wall next to Jenny, his bound hands on his pulled-up knees.

Wearily resting his forehead against the rough ropes, he said in a voice too low to be heard by anyone but Jenny, "This is all my fault! I was so sure Estrella was our friend . . . If only I hadn't believed her!"

"She fooled the rest of us, too—even Steve!" Jenny whispered back.

That wasn't quite true, but Justin felt better. Jenny really was a great sister, he thought gratefully. She never rubbed it in when a guy was wrong.

His thoughts were interrupted as Steve whispered urgently into the darkness, "Mr. Parker, we've got to get out of here tonight!"

He added, still in a whisper. "Mr. Parker, I wasn't bluffing about the danger. I figure we don't have more than a day before that melt-off comes shooting down this canyon. We've got to get to high ground!"

Uncle Pete was silent, but Jenny whispered, "How can we escape? We're all tied up!"

"Yeah, and what about the guards?" Justin added quietly.

Steve's low voice suddenly carried a note of amusement. "I picked up a few tricks in the Marines. I can be out of these ropes in ten minutes. As for the guards . . . well, it's pitch dark. This band is pretty amateur. It wouldn't be hard to evade them. How about it, Mr. Parker? Are you willing to try?"

There was a moment's silence, then Uncle Pete answered slowly, "Lieutenant Cardoza, I think you do have an excellent chance of getting out of here. But we aren't trained soldiers. We can't move as quietly or as quickly as you can. They'll be checking on us, and once they discover our escape, they'll be after us in a second. We'd just slow you down."

Steve sighed. "I'm aware of that. But I'm willing to risk it if you are."

"No!" Uncle Pete whispered decisively. "Our chances of escape are too small. And if we failed, we'd never get another chance. You'd better go for help. We'll cover for you here."

Steve sounded relieved. "That's probably the best plan. I'll go as soon as the camp is quiet. It'll take me a few hours to get to a main road, but I should have help here by morning."

He broke off abruptly at the sound of voices approaching the tent. The tent flap opened, the distant glimmer of the campfire making only a slight difference in the darkness. A small figure slipped in. Justin heard a thump, and the sound of a striking match—then the red-yellow flicker of a candle lit Estrella's unhappy face.

"Justin! Jenny!" The candle dripped wax and sent long,

wavering shadows across the tent floor as Estrella leaned down to pick up the bundle she had dropped. "I knew you would be cold so I brought you some blankets."

Seeing their bound hands and feet, Estrella set down the candle. Shaking out the pile of heavy wool blankets, she carefully draped a blanket around each of the prisoners.

"Thanks a lot, Estrella," Jenny said gratefully as Estrella tucked her blanket close.

Uncle Pete and Steve, on the side of the tent opposite the twins, nodded their thanks. But Justin, snuggling into his own blanket, just said grudgingly, "While you're in here, why don't you do something useful—like untie our hands!"

"No!" Justin wondered if he had imagined the sudden look of fright on Estrella's face. Then she frowned. "No, I cannot let you go!"

"Yeah, I forgot you're one of them!" Justin answered sarcastically. "Why don't you just go away and leave us alone!"

Instead of leaving, Estrella squatted down in front of Justin and Jenny. "Please, I know you are angry with me. I . . . I don't want you to hate me. I want to explain."

Pushing back the long hair that fell over her slim shoulders, she pleaded, "Carlos did tell me to be your friend. And he told me to bring you here. You see, Carlos and my 'family' have done everything for me. How could I say no when they needed my help?"

"Yeah, so you pretended you needed friends—that you really like us!" Justin interrupted with a growl. "You sure fooled me!"

"But I was not pretending! . . . Well, perhaps at first . . ." Estrella's low voice shook a little. "When I knew you—how you loved each other even when you quarreled, how you were kind to me when I am not even of your country—then it wasn't pretend anymore. I was glad to be your friend. And when I saw how sad you were about your uncle, I was very sorry."

"You call this being a friend?" Justin growled. He lowered his voice as Uncle Pete and Steve looked in their direction. "Carlos is planning to kill us tomorrow if you don't get your men back!"

Estrella looked surprised. "But I told you already that no one will be hurt. Carlos just talks that way to make the police let Eduardo and Paco go. They promised me that they would not hurt you if I brought you here. No matter what happens, you and your uncle will be released unharmed."

She added soothingly, "So you see, there is nothing to worry about. Now you will stop being angry and be my friend, will you not?"

Jenny looked doubtful as Estrella stopped speaking, but Justin was furious. Looking hard at the young guerrilla girl, he whispered sarcastically, "Do you really think we're stupid enough to fall for your lies again? Did Carlos send you in here? Does he think we'll tell you our escape plans or something if you're nice to us?"

Estella's chin went up proudly. Leaning forward, she hissed, "You talk about God and forgiveness—but do you forgive?"

Justin didn't answer, and she jumped to her feet so fast that she bumped her head on the ridge pole of the tent. They had been talking too softly for the adults to overhear, but now Estrella almost shouted, "I should have known better than to be friends with you! *You* are the liars—like all Americans!"

She grabbed the candlestick and turned to storm out of the tent when Steve called out quietly, "Speaking of Americans, I found out what happened to your father."

Estrella froze, then turned around slowly. Justin exclaimed

with sudden interest, "So you did check it out! That's great!" He glanced at Estrella, and his excitement turned into a scowl.

"That's right! I checked the embassy records for a Gary Adams traveling from Bogota to the U.S. that year, and then ran his name through the Interpol computer."

Looking up at Estrella, he said gently, "Your father never did leave you, Estrella. He was in a car accident in Miami and was killed instantly. He didn't have any close relatives in the U.S., and I guess the insurance company that settled everything didn't know he had a wife and daughter in Colombia."

"My father didn't leave me?" Estrella looked dazed. Shaking her head, she whispered, "I . . . I have hated him for so long! I went with Carlos because I hated him."

"Yes, I know," Steve said gently. "You joined the guerrillas because they were fighting those so-called rich men like your father who would leave a little girl out in the streets to starve."

"And all the time he was . . . !" Estrella suddenly whirled around. The candle dropped unnoticed to the floor and went out as she plunged through the tent flap.

Justin was blinking his eyes in the sudden darkness when Jenny spoke up quietly. "Justin, don't you think you were a little hard on Estrella?"

"I don't want to talk about it!" he muttered. Rolling over on his side, he nestled into his blanket. Faint rustlings told him that the others were also trying to get comfortable. Only the occasional twitter of a bird settling down for the night and the chirping of crickets disturbed the sleeping camp.

Justin stared into the darkness. At least his angry thoughts took his mind from the gnawing hunger pains and growing discomfort in his bound arms and legs.

She lied to us! he told himself fiercely.

That was what really hurt. He had trusted Estrella—given her his friendship—and now they were all in great danger because of her. He didn't believe for one minute that those hard-eyed men and women around the campfire had any intention of letting them go as easily as Estrella claimed.

He tried to get to sleep, but somehow Estrella's angry words echoed in his mind, *"You talk about God and forgiveness! You are the liars . . . the liars . . . the liars!"*

"Stop moving around!" Jenny said crossly. "I'm trying to sleep!"

Justin lay still and finally dozed off. It seemed only minutes later that he was disturbed by a movement at the end of the tent. A firm hand touched his shoulder.

"I'm leaving now." Justin could hardly hear Steve's whisper. "I've left my blanket humped up in case the guard looks in before morning. I'm sorry I have to leave you tied up, but it's better they think you don't know anything about my escape."

Soundlessly, he dropped to the floor of the tent. Justin sensed rather than heard Steve lift the canvas wall of the tent just enough to thrust his head and shoulders through. He lay flat on his stomach for a long moment. Justin knew that Steve was scanning the area, checking for guards. Then, without a whisper of a noise, Steve was gone.

Chapter 10

Danger in the Canyon

Justin awoke coughing. Lying on his side, his head pillowed on something hard, he wondered for a moment where he was. He shifted position, and a twinge of pain shot up his numb arms and legs. Instantly, the events of the last few days flooded into his mind. He now realized that a sharp rock under the canvas beneath his head was digging into his ear.

He struggled to a sitting position, noticing that the wool blanket had slipped from his shoulders. Although the mountain dawn usually was bitterly cold, the air seemed strangely warm and thick. He breathed in deeply and almost choked as the biting smell of sulfur burned his lungs. Outside, a rooster—probably destined for the big cooking pot Justin had seen the day before—announced the dawn, and the first light began to replace the darkness inside the tent.

Justin had been awakened twice during the night as a guard briefly flashed a powerful flashlight around the tent. The guard had done no more than glance at the humped-up blanket that marked the spot where Steve had been. Cold fear suddenly struck Justin's empty stomach as he realized that Steve hadn't returned yet. The guard would check again any minute now. In full daylight, he would have to notice that one of his prisoners had escaped.

Beside him, Jenny stirred and sat up. She grimaced, cautiously moving her bound arms and legs, then bent over in a sudden coughing fit. At the sound, Uncle Pete too raised his head from where he leaned in a sitting position against the side of the tent. His keen eyes took in his wide-awake nephew and niece.

"Well, kids," he said softly, "it looks like Steve didn't make it back."

"Yeah, and smell the air!" Justin answered. "We've got to get out of here!"

"What are we going to do, Uncle Pete?" Jenny asked anxiously.

Before Uncle Pete could answer, the tent flap lifted. But instead of the guard they expected, Estrella slipped in, a sharp knife in her hand. Justin turned his head away as she knelt to saw at his bonds.

Estrella explained briefly, "You will not need these during the day. I will take you down to the river to wash. Then there will be something to eat."

As the ropes binding Justin's hands and ankles fell to the ground, she turned to Jenny, who smiled at her in her usual friendly fashion. Estrella didn't smile back. She looked as though she hadn't slept. She cut through the first strand of the rope that bound Jenny's ankles. "We must hurry. It looks like a bad storm is coming."

She glanced over Jenny's shoulder at the other end of the tent, and the black-fringed, blue eyes widened in sudden horror. The knife dropped from her hand as she demanded,

"Where is Steve? Where did he go?"

Fear pinched her thin features as she grabbed frantically at the heaped-up blanket that had taken Steve's place. "No, he can't be gone!"

Forgetting her errand, she ran from the tent. Justin grabbed at the knife and finished sawing through the half-cut rope, then freed Uncle Pete. Rubbing at swollen hands, Uncle Pete said soberly, "There's going to be trouble, kids. I wish you were out of this, but it's too late now."

He looked steadily at the two of them. "I don't know how much more time we have, but there's one thing we can do right now. Let's pray."

Bowing his head, Justin nodded in agreement as Uncle Pete prayed for Steve's safety, and that he would bring help soon. But he opened his eyes in shock when Uncle Pete added, "Help us to be Your witness to our captors. They too need Your love."

They don't need love, Justin thought bitterly. *They need punishment—especially Estrella!*

Angry shouts arose outside the tent. Lifting his head, Uncle Pete said quickly in a low voice, "No matter what happens, kids, don't forget that God is in control of every situation— even this one!"

Just then, the tent flap was yanked back. The guerrilla who had stood guard all night thrust his head through the opening. His black eyes narrowed with anger as he caught sight of Steve's empty blanket. Shoving his rifle through the flap, he angrily motioned for the three Parkers to step out-side.

The dawn was slowly lightening the steel-gray of the sky as they emerged from the tent, but there would be no sun that morning. The air was not so heavy out here, but a sharp smell of suflur still burned Justin's nostrils if he breathed in too deeply.

Justin thought at first it was fog that shrouded the camp with ghostly white. But as he scuffed a sneaker against the ground, he realized that the ground, the tents, and even the trees were cloaked with a thick layer of gray-white dust.

Ash! he thought grimly. *It's coming down faster!*

The guerrilla leader was over by the picnic table talking to Estrella, the rapid motions of his hands expressing his anger. Estrella looked upset. Breaking off at the sight of the Parkers, Carlos marched over and struck Uncle Pete hard across the face.

"Where is the American spy? How has he escaped?" he demanded angrily.

Rubbing his bruised face, Uncle Pete answered evenly, "I don't know. I was asleep."

The ring of truth in his voice seemed to convince Carlos, and he turned his hot, angry gaze toward the twins. Justin was afraid that the leader would question him, but after a long, searching glance, Carlos turned to the guard who still stood there, his rifle trained on the small group of hostages.

"Imbecile!" he shouted. The guard backed up, fear on his dark face, as Carlos switched to angry Spanish. The young guerrilla was trembling by the time Carlos stopped shouting, and Justin wondered what threat could have frightened him so.

Ignoring the guard, Carlos turned again to Uncle Pete. "You knew of this escape, did you not?"

Uncle Pete faced the guerrilla leader steadily. "Yes, I knew he would try to escape. He knew this place was dangerous and he didn't want to be caught in this canyon when the eruption hit."

Uncle Pete reached out a hand and rubbed it against the tent. His fingers came away coated silvery white. "Can't you see he was telling the truth? You must at least move to high ground!"

Estrella moved to Carlos' side and whispered urgently. The guerrilla leader glanced at the strange gray cast of the sky, then reached out and fingered the ash. "There is often ash in these mountains, but we will move out."

Justin gave a sigh of relief, then froze as Carlos gave him a cold, dark stare. "Do not think this will help you escape! If the American spy should now make his way back, we will not be here."

Motioning toward his hostages, he snapped at Estrella, "Tell the others to begin packing up at once. Then take care of these."

Estrella was back within seconds. She led the Parkers to a crude outhouse, then down to the river to wash, the guard—a different one this time—staying a few feet behind, machine gun ready. Justin scowled to see Jenny chatting quietly with Estrella as they completed a quick wash without soap or towels. Jenny might be softening toward Estrella, but he, Justin, wasn't about to let the young guerrilla girl fool him again!

The camp was already swarming with activity by the time they walked back from the river. The tents were now flat on the ground, and the guard motioned for Uncle Pete to sit nearby, with his back against a tree near the edge of the river. Perching on a large boulder, the guard cradled his gun across his knees. His black eyes didn't move for an instant from Uncle Pete's face, but when Estrella said something to him in Spanish, he nodded and allowed her to lead the twins over to the campfire.

A sizzling smell of something frying twisted Justin's stomach with hunger. Several of the guerrillas were still eating, huddled close to the warmth of the fire. Justin's mouth watered as Estrella handed him an enamel plate piled high with cakes made of finely-ground corn about the size of pancakes, but much thicker. Each was sliced and stuffed with a fried egg.

"Arepas," Estrella said, putting an enamel mug in his other hand. Justin growled a reluctant thanks as he took a sip of the strong, sweet *cafe con leche* (coffee with milk) he had already learned to enjoy. Estrella handed Jenny her food, then hurried away with a plate and mug for Uncle Pete.

Squatting down by the fire, Justin hurriedly chewed one of the thick corn cakes. Biting into her own *arepa,* Jenny looked across the clearing to watch Estrella carry a bundle of blankets over to a pack mule.

Swallowing, she demanded, "Justin, do you have to be so mean to Estrella? You're hurting her feelings!"

"So what?" Justin growled, stuffing the rest of the *arepa* into his mouth. "She's done a lot worse than that to us!"

Jenny looked exasperated. "Justin, you are so stubborn! You make up your mind about something, and nothing can change it! Like Estrella—at first, you decided she was our friend, so you wouldn't listen when I warned you about her."

Suddenly hurt, Justin snapped, "I already said I was sorry! I was wrong! She had me fooled. What more do you want?"

To Justin's surprise, Jenny answered thoughtfully, "I don't think you were wrong! I think she's telling the truth. She really did want to be our friend—at least after she got to know us. You *felt* that—that's why you were so sure she wouldn't hurt us."

She made a helpless motion with her coffee mug. "You know what I mean! I can't explain it very well. Anyway, the only mistake you made was thinking she couldn't be our friend and still lie to us about Uncle Pete and all this. She really believes these guys aren't going to hurt us—and maybe she's right!"

She leaned forward, waving an *arepa* right under his nose. "But that isn't the point! The point is, now you've decided that Estrella is a jerk and our worst enemy, so you've made up your mind to hate her for the rest of your life. And you're not going to let anyone change your mind about that either! Mom always says you're so 'sensible' and 'determined.' Well, I think you're just plain pig-headed!"

Justin set his jaw stubbornly and refused to answer, but his sister's words had hit home. He knew that holding grudges was one of his worst faults. For the first time, he began to wonder what he would have done if he'd been in Estrella's shoes—and his anger slowly began to ebb away.

Justin felt much better with a stomach full of *arepas* and *cafe con leche*. He couldn't quite smile when Estrella collected their dishes, but he didn't scowl either.

It was beginning to drizzle as the twins walked back to join Uncle Pete, and a strong wind stung Justin's face with what felt like blowing sand. In spite of the drizzle, the still-falling ash was beginning to give the camp the look of a silvery Christmas card. A tiny pebble struck Justin's back as he ducked under the shelter of the trees. Others followed, hitting the ground like a shower of tiny hailstones.

"It won't be long now!" Uncle Pete commented as Justin and Jenny squatted beside him. His expression was as calm as ever, but Justin knew he was worried as he looked up at the canyon and murmured, "Where could Steve be?"

Carlos shouted angrily, and the guerrillas began to work faster. The tents had been rolled into bundles, and two of the guerrillas were leading pack mules up the steep path to the top of the gully when a shout caught Justin's attention. It was Alejandro, and Justin suddenly realized that he hadn't seen the young guerrilla at all that morning.

Alejandro jumped out of the way of a pack mule and ran into camp. Carlos strode over, asking a sharp question in Spanish. Alejandro shook his head and poured out an answering flood of words. Justin caught his breath at the look on Carlos' face as he snapped a sharp response, then marched over to the three hostages.

Uncle Pete rose to his feet as Carlos announced coldly, "Your embassy has not done as we demanded. Our men have not been released. Now we are out of time. If the American spy finds his way back, this place will be filled soon with soldiers."

He looked at Uncle Pete thoughtfully. "Do you truly think that your people will not give in to our request? Even if you write and demand it?"

Uncle Pete's gaze was steady as he answered firmly, "My embassy will not give in to terrorist demands, no matter how long you wait. And I wouldn't want them to give in to threats for my sake."

The guerrilla leader turned somber eyes on the twins. "And what about your family? Would you risk their lives just to keep two of my men in jail?"

Uncle Pete sighed heavily as he too glanced down at the listening children. "You know I would do anything to protect Justin and Jenny. But it doesn't make any differnce. Even if I could persuade my embassy to deal with you, your own government would refuse to release the prisoners. Why don't you just let us go and be done with it all!"

Carlos didn't answer. Justin held his breath as the guerrillas' leader stared at them for a long moment. Then, shrugging his shoulders as though he had made a decision, he walked away and shouted an order.

The last of the guerrillas, backpacks over their shoulders, began to move up the narrow trail to the top of the gully. Within moments, the campsite was abandoned, except for the Parkers and their guard. The shower of stones and ash was growing heavier, and Justin and Jenny followed Uncle Pete further into the shelter of the cluster of trees.

Carlos walked over, his own machine gun slung across his back and a pistol in a holster at his side. Alejandro came behind him, carrying a coil of nylon rope. He motioned to their guard, and he too headed toward the cliff.

Justin jumped to his feet, relieved that they were at last moving out. When Alejandro began roping his hands together in front of him, he wasn't surprised. The guerrillas were obviously making sure that they wouldn't escape along the way. Alejandro moved along to Jenny and Uncle Pete, quickly looping the same rope around their wrists and pulling it tightly.

Carlos stopped in front of Uncle Pete. "I thought you would wish to know that the American spy was right. We have just heard on the radio that the volcano is again melting the snow on the Nevada del Ruiz. They were careful to announce that no towns or *haciendas* are in danger."

He gave a sign to Alejandro. Then, to Justin's shock, Alejandro looped the remainder of the long rope around a low limb of the tree. He yanked it so hard that their hands were pulled overhead.

"What are you doing?" Uncle Pete demanded sternly. "If you've heard that the snow is melting, then you know there will be floods through these canyons. Tie us up and leave us at the top of the gully if you aren't taking us with you. But don't leave us here!"

Carlos just turned and walked away. Alejandro gave them a nasty grin and made a taunting remark in Spanish, then began knotting the rope tightly to the branch. Realizing with horror just what Carlos had in mind, Justin kicked Alejandro sharply in the shins. Alejandro kicked back, knocking Justin's feet out from under him. The ropes cut deeply into his wrists as he struggled to regain his footing. Alejandro tied a final knot, then walked away.

Justin glanced up at the cliff face. Estrella was halfway up, a heavy bundle on her back. He shouted bitterly, "So your friends won't hurt anyone, Estrella? So much for your promises!"

Justin's shout brought Estrella to a halt. Even at that distance, he could see the horror on her face as she took in the situation. A moment later, she had dropped her bundle and was flying down the path. Carlos had stooped to pick up a last small bundle of personal items. Estrella rushed at him, screaming, "What are you doing? You cannot leave them here!"

Carlos only paused to swing his pack to his shoulders as he answered loud enough for the Parkers to hear clearly, "Why should we leave witnesses?"

"But you promised not to hurt them!" Estrella pounded him on the chest with her small fists as she shouted, "You cannot leave them here! They will die!"

The guerrilla leader grabbed her wrists, raising his voice. "Do not be stupid! The government will not exchange our men even for three of them. They are no good to us now. They would just slow us down."

Estrella broke away. She flew at the knots, trying to untie them as she cried, "They did promise not to hurt you! They did! Please believe me! I did not know they would do this! Please forgive me!"

As Carlos pulled her away, Jenny answered softly, "We do believe you, Estrella. Don't worry. We'll be all right! Maybe the eruption won't even come here."

Uncle Pete said quietly, "You'd better go, Estrella. Your friends are waiting for you."

"No, I won't go! Not until Carlos lets you go!"

Carlos grabbed Estrella by the arm. "You will do as you are told! You, at least, are still of some use to us!"

He lapsed into Spanish as he forced her across the clearing. Estrella looked back pleadingly, and Justin suddenly knew that he had something to do before it was too late.

"Estrella!" he called. Estrella stopped in spite of Carlos' scowl and iron grip, and Justin added, "I'm sorry I was so mad at you, Estrella. I *do* forgive you!"

Estrella didn't answer. She stood for a moment with her head bowed, and Justin realized with shock that she was crying. With a Spanish curse, Carlos pulled her away. She didn't look back again as he pushed her up the trail. Moments later, the path and the cliff top above were empty, and the Parkers were alone.

"Okay, kids," Uncle Pete said. "Let's figure out a way to get out of this mess."

Fifteen minutes later, Justin admitted to himself that there might not be a way out. They had tried to loosen the rope, but Alejandro had tied the knots too well, and the branch over which he had hung the rope was well out of reach of even Uncle Pete's outstretched arms. Uncle Pete encouraged the two children, even making jokes as they stumbled over each other in an attempt to free their upstretched hands, but Justin saw that the cheerful smile that split the red-gold beard didn't reach his somber eyes.

Justin couldn't see his watch, but he guessed that it was about mid-morning. The shower of rocks had slowly dwindled away, and even the ash-fall was lessening. The sky grew a shade less gray. Relaxing a moment against his burning wrists, Justin caught the faint roar of a distant waterfall. His spirits began to lift.

"Maybe the eruption is over," he declared with relief. "Nothing has happened after all. Maybe we can just wait for Steve to show up. He should be here any minute." He didn't let himself even wonder if something might have happened to Steve.

Uncle Pete shook his head. "It isn't the volcano we have to worry about—it's the runoff. Whether the eruption is over or not, that water and mud will still be heading down these canyons."

He looked down. "See if you can find something we can use to cut us loose."

As Justin scanned the ground at his feet, Jenny cried triumphantly, "Look! There's a broken pop bottle!"

The shard of glass lay against the side of the tree trunk. Jenny was closest. "Try to kick it over here!" Uncle Pete said urgently.

But Jenny couldn't quite reach it. "Just a minute! I'll take my shoes off." In seconds, she had kicked off one sneaker and wriggled out of a sock.

"You'll cut yourself," Justin protested as Jenny tried to grab the broken bottle between two toes.

"I don't think that really matters right now," she panted. Finally successful, Jenny began pulling the piece of broken bottle slowly toward her.

Justin's eyes were glued on the shard of glass slowly

moving toward them, when he suddenly realized that the waterfall sound he had heard earlier had grown much louder and seemed to be closer. Justin raised his head. He stared upstream in disbelief, and a desperate fear wrapped around his lungs.

Still far up the gully, its gray-brown mass squeezed almost to the top of the sheer cliff tops by the narrow stone sides of the canyon, was a solid, moving wall of rock and mud. Justin watched in helpless horror as the *lahar* spawned by the Nevada del Ruiz swept relentlessly down toward the camp.

Chapter 11

Unexpected Help

The far-off mass of mud and ice was still hardly visible against the dirt-brown color of the canyon walls. It seemed to move so slowly that Justin wondered momentarily if he was mistaken. He glanced over at his sister, who had just managed to grab the piece of broken bottle between both feet. When he looked back up, he was shocked to see how much the wall of mud had grown in just that split-second of time.

A gasp beside him as Jenny dropped the piece of glass told Justin that she too had noticed the swelling wave of mud. Panicking, Justin yanked hopelessly at the ropes that stretched his arms upward, ignoring the sharp pain as the twisted strands cut into his wrists. He heard the frightened sobs of his sister, but there was no time for words.

The rush of a waterfall rose to the rumble of a mountainsized cement mixer as the churning mass of boulders and mud grew with every breath. Justin caught sight of the massive roots of an uprooted evergreen giant tossed onto the crest of the wave like a broken twig.

He sagged against the ropes, not bothering to struggle further. He was past feeling any fear. He spared a brief thought for his parents—they would be so sad when they heard the news. Then he bowed his head and whispered quietly, "Dear God, I guess it'd take a miracle to get us out of this one!"

Then it happened—so suddenly he was sure he had imagined it. A soft voice spoke in his ear, "Come! We must leave here!"

He lifted his head to see Estrella standing on tiptoes in front of him. Her face was tense with fear, but she was already reaching up to saw at the ropes that twisted around his wrists.

"Estrella!" he cried, his shout jerking Uncle Pete and Jenny around. "You came back!"

Estrella didn't stop sawing for a second, but she gasped, "I could not leave you here. I ran away from the others."

The knife she held was an old—and dull—kitchen knife. She had sawed only part way through the knotted strands, and sweat already beaded on her forehead. Justin glanced at the approaching wave of *lahar*. It was much closer now, and no longer looked solid. His sharp eyes could pick out the boulders, branches, even dead animals that dotted the heaving, slick surface of the mud.

"Estrella!" he cried urgently. "It's too late! Save yourself!"

"No!" Estrella cried, sawing harder. "I will not leave you again!"

"Then just cut this rope up here!" Uncle Pete shouted over the churning rumble of the advancing mud. He motioned with his head toward the single strand that stretched their arms up toward the branch just above his hands. "If you cut this, the rest of the ropes will fall off."

Estrella rushed to Uncle Pete's side, but the rope was well over her head and out of reach. In an instant, she managed to roll a small boulder up beside him. Perching on it, she began to saw frantically, still straining to reach the rope. The towering, gray-brown wall had now reached a thick belt of cypress and tamarack trees that lined the riverbed only half a mile upstream. Justin held his breath as they were broken off and smashed under the relentless movement of the *lahar*. Within seconds they were gone, and thousands of tons of mud, ice, and debris pushed through the bottleneck of the narrow canyon into the wider valley which spread on down the mountainside.

It was this that gave them hope. The mad rush of the oncoming river of mud slowed a little as it spread out to fill every nook and cranny of the now broader gully. And at that moment, Estrella's knife broke through the rope. The strands that had been so tight instantly loosened, and the Parkers quickly shook off the ropes.

"Come on!" Estrella cried, her voice tight with fear. She began sprinting toward the cliff, the others close behind. Jenny paused long enough to snatch up shoes and socks, but her long legs shot her past both Justin and Estrella.

Running faster than he ever had in his life, Justin glanced upstream. The wave of *lahar* had dropped in height as it spread out sideways into the valley and spilled over the lower far bank of the gully. But it was now so close that it loomed high over the small, running figures, blotting out the skyline. Justin reached the bottom of the cliff right behind his uncle and Jenny. Estrella, still out of breath from her run to save them, had fallen slightly behind.

The path which they had been herded down the day before was nothing more than a narrow trail carved out of the cliff face by generations of wild animals. Steep enough that climbers occasionally had to use hands to pull themselves up, it was hardly wide enough for one person. Uncle Pete was already climbing rapidly, his powerful hand yanking Jenny up behind him.

The river of mud was still dropping in height. It was now a race to see if they could climb far enough up the path to escape the reach of the thundering wave as it swept past.

Justin scrambled faster. He kicked his foot loose from a tangled root system that, washed free by mountain rains, was spread out across the path. He grabbed at a clump of grass as he lost his balance. He sure didn't remember this trail having so many obstacles on the way down! Uncle Pete and Jenny were now yards above him.

A sudden scream rose above the deafening roar of the oncoming torrent. Justin glanced backward. Right behind him, Estrella lay flat on her stomach, her foot caught in the root system that had just tripped him. He saw her tug frantically at the root that trapped her, sobbing with fear, but she couldn't pull free. He hesitated only a split second.

"No!" Estrella cried as she saw him turn back, "Don't stop!"

The *lahar* had almost reached them, and the heaving, churning gray-brown mass still reared yards above their heads. Already Justin felt the moisture that splashed ahead of the wave. There was no time to think.

Reaching down, Justin tugged at the root with all the force he could manage, allowing Estrella to pull her foot free. Then, with a single motion, he pulled the still-sobbing girl to her feet and pushed her ahead of him up the trail.

There was only time to take three steps. They had almost made it. It was the very crest of the wave that Justin saw sweeping over them. He gave Estrella a powerful shove up the path, then grabbed for an overhanging branch. He managed to gulp a lung-full of air, then the *lahar* passed over his head.

It was much colder than Justin had imagined. He had forgotten that the river of mud fed from the melted snow and ice of the Andean glaciers. He was so cold that he hardly felt the branches, rocks, and other debris that battered his body. Holding his breath and keeping his eyes squeezed shut, he clung to the branch with all his strength, fighting the relentless pressure that tried to pull him downstream.

Long seconds passed before the level of the *lahar* dropped enough that he could pull his head out of the mud. Shaking his head hard to clear the mud from his eyes, he glimpsed Estrella just beyond him, clinging to an overhanging tree as the mud flow washed her up to the waist.

He had just raised his head to search for his sister and uncle when he felt a movement under his hands. A heavy branch had slammed into the stunted juniper he clung to, tearing it away from the cliff side. Before he could grab for another hold, Justin was swept out into the icy, sticky, racing river of *lahar*.

Justin's eyes were still filmed over with mud, but he caught a brief, misty glimpse of three figures on the part of the path that was still visible. At least the other three had made it! The screams of the two girls rose above the roaring in his ears as he was carried helplessly down the valley.

Justin kicked to stay afloat, struggling wildly to keep his head out of the mud. Something nudged at his legs, then he caught sight of a branching set of antlers as a dead deer swept by him.

He no longer felt so cold. In fact, he didn't really feel

anything anymore—not even his arms and legs. The mud oozed up over his mouth. His head felt as heavy as lead, and it seemed it would be so easy just to let himself slip down into the mud. He was so tired!

He hardly felt the bump. Lifting his head with an effort, he saw a log as long as his body floating beside him. Moving along at the same speed as he was, it seemed to be lying still. The broken branches that still extended from the log kept it from rolling. Bunching up numb, exhausted muscles, Justin grabbed for the log just as a sudden wave crashed over his head.

The wave receded, leaving Justin choking. Blinking the mud once more from his eyes, Justin gratefully draped his arms across a couple of branches and rested his weary head against the log. As long as he could hold on, he still had a chance of getting out of this.

A jolt brought his head up. The log had bumped into something large and bulky. Under the coat of sticky gray-brown, Justin made out faint black and white markings, then a long head. It was a Holstein cow that probably had wandered away from some highland farm and was taking a drink at the river's edge when the *lahar* struck.

Justin thought it too was dead until a low moo protested helplessly. He caught a glimpse of pleading, large brown eyes, then a sudden undertow pulled the cow below the surface of the mud. Justin held tightly to the log, fighting the pull of the undertow. The next time he looked up, the cow was gone.

As the mud flow spread down into the widening gully, the cliff top dropped until now it was no more than a high bank running along one edge of the valley. The other side of the valley now stretched out flat into a heavily forested plateau. As the *lahar* spread out across the plateau, the river slowed even further.

There seemed to be currents in the mud flow, because the log Justin clung to had begun to drift toward the high bank. Justin heard a shout and eased his head to one side. Three distant figures were racing along the edge of the gully.

He heard a deep call. "Justin! Are you all right?"

Justin raised a leaden arm in answer to the call, and heard a glad shout in response. He could now make out his uncle running along the edge. With new strength, he tried to kick himself closer to the shore. There were branches and trees growing there, and he might still be able to pull himself out.

But just at that moment a new force grabbed at him with an iron grip. He felt himself being carried away from the bank as some undercurrent swung him around in a vast circle. He clung desperately to the log as it whirled around, faster and faster.

A whirlpool! he thought faintly. *I'll never get out of this!*

He had just enough time to take a deep breath before the whirlpool sucked him under the heaving, rolling surface. Clutching frantically at the broken branches of the log, he felt himself pulled down, down. He couldn't even kick against the immense weight of the icy mud that pressed him from all sides.

He couldn't feel whether his numb fingers still clung to the log. He was desperately fighting the urge to breathe when a blinding pain struck across the side of his head. A burst of fireworks exploded somewhere behind his eyelids, then everything went black.

Chapter 12

Rescued or ... ?

From far away down a long, dark tunnel, Justin heard the murmur of voices. He knew something had happened, but he couldn't remember what. He knew he should get up . . . find the voices . . . but he was too tired to move.

The voices came nearer. This time he caught the words.

"Will he be all right, Uncle Pete?" It was the tearful voice of his sister. "He's so cold!"

"He's breathing, anyway," answered Uncle Pete heavily. Justin could hear the worry underlying the steady voice. "He needs blankets and a warm bed."

He tried to open his eyes, to tell them he was fine, but his tongue felt heavy and his eyes were glued shut. He felt something wet against his face. The weight lifted from his eyes, and he opened them slowly.

A somewhat blurry Estrella bent over him, holding a handkerchief that still dripped muddy water. As his vision slowly focused, she leaned closer. Seeing his open eyes, she cried out joyfully, "He is awake!"

Uncle Pete's face swam into view. His hazel eyes were full of concern, but the red-brown beard smiled as he asked calmly, "Justin, are you all right?"

Justin attempted a nod, but a sharp pain shot through his head as he moved, and he shut his eyes again. He tried to speak, but he couldn't seem to pry his mouth open. He felt Estrella's handkerchief again and realized it was mud that choked him.

"Don't try to get up!" Uncle Pete ordered firmly. Justin felt his uncle's big hands moving expertly over his arms and legs. He winced as Uncle Pete touched a sore spot on the side of his head.

"Doesn't look like anything is broken," Uncle Pete said at last in a relieved voice. "He'll have a good collection of scrapes and bruises, and he's got a nasty bump on the side of his head. He must have banged it against something."

Justin opened his eyes again. This time, everything stayed in focus. He turned his head slowly. He was lying on a grassy bank. The numbness was leaving his body, and he began to shiver violently.

Uncle Pete moved to tuck a jacket closer around him. Looking up, he saw that neither Uncle Pete nor the girls wore their jackets. Uncle Pete was without a shirt as well. Cautiously turning his head again, he saw his own mudsoaked jeans, shirt, and jacket stretched over a branch. Uncle Pete's mud-streaked, once-white shirt was tossed over a bush. He had obviously used it to towel Justin dry.

Estrella knelt beside Justin, her face tear-streaked. "You should not have come back for me! You could have been killed!"

The drying mud crackled on Justin's cheeks as he grinned weakly. "Look who's talking!"

A thin, smoky haze still hid the sun, but it was no longer cold. Gradually, Justin stopped shivering and began to feel warm under the blanket of jackets. He tried to sit up, and this time Uncle Pete didn't stop him. Uncle Pete helped him prop himself against a tree trunk, and he sat quietly until the world stopped turning circles around him.

He looked out over the bank. A gray-brown lake now filled the entire valley as far as he could see. He suddenly remembered the whirlpool pulling him down into darkness. "What happened?" he asked faintly, one hand on his still-aching head. "How . . . how did I get here?"

Uncle Pete picked up the jacket that had tumbled from his shoulders, and tucked it back around him. "Well, as soon as you were swept away, we got up to the top of the cliff and started running downsteam. We finally saw you holding onto that log. When you waved, we knew you were alive. Then, when your log started swinging toward the bank, I climbed down, hoping to cut you off."

His expression was suddenly bleak. "I almost had you, but you swung away again and then . . . you just disappeared! We thought you were gone."

"It was a whirlpool," Justin murmured, suddenly shivering again. "But how did I get out?"

"You were under for quite some time," Uncle Pete continued. "At least it seemed like it. Then, all of a sudden you popped up again—still holding on to that log. The whirlpool must have tossed you to the surface. We couldn't tell if you were alive or not. You swung around in a wide circle. On the second time around, you came close enough for me to grab you."

Justin suddenly noticed that Uncle Pete too was covered with the gray, slimy mud from the waist down. You were unconscious, but I managed to grab you before you were dragged away again. The current was so strong, I was afraid both of us would be swept downstream. But Jenny and Estrella here helped me get you up on the bank."

Jenny dropped down onto the grass beside her brother. She too was tear-streaked, but she was grinning as she gave him a hard hug. "You sure scared us, Justin. I can't believe we're all alive! And we've got Uncle Pete back, too!"

Uncle Pete's calm voice broke into her jubilation. "God certainly had His mighty hand around us today, kids! Let's stop and thank Him now."

The sudden snap of a breaking branch brought Justin's bowed head up with a jerk. His heart sank as three armed men quickly surrounded the little group under the tree.

Chapter 13

Homeward Bound

Unlike the band of guerrillas that had held them hostage, these men were neatly dressed in complete camouflage uniforms. But their machine guns looked as well-kept as those of the guerrillas, and they obviously knew how to use them.

Their dark eyes were cold and watchful as Uncle Pete and the girls slowly rose to their feet, their arms in the air. Justin, covered up by three jackets but dressed only in his boxer shorts, decided to stay where he was.

One of the men barked a question in Spanish, and Justin saw that Estrella looked both angry and afraid as she reluctantly answered. *Here we go again!* he thought wearily.

But just at that moment an impatient, familiar voice snapped an order in Spanish, and the three soldiers' cold frowns turned to smiles. Justin dropped his arms with a sigh of relief as Marine Lieutenant Steve Cardoza, looking as tough and competent as ever, stepped into the clearing.

"Steve!" Jenny was already running toward the broad-shouldered Marine. Glancing sharply around the group, Steve looked relieved to see that they were all there. He eyed Estrella with surprise, but made no comment.

Jenny threw her arms around him with her usual enthusiasm. "We thought something had happened to you!"

Uncle Pete too stepped forward, drying mud crinkling on his bare chest and pants as he said, "Glad to see you made it through safely."

"And am I ever glad to see *you* all made it!" Steve said with a grin as he rumpled Jenny's hair. A small bandage ran across one side of his forehead where the guerrilla had struck him, but he was looking very fit again, and not at all as though he had hiked most of the night.

His expression was suddenly serious as he turned to stare out over the steep bank. "At first, I thought we were too late!"

"What *took* you so long?" Jenny demanded. "You should have been back *hours* ago!"

Steve dropped to the grass beside Justin and asked, "Are you okay, kid?"

When Justin nodded, he turned back to Jenny. "Well, it wasn't as easy to get help as I'd hoped. It took me several hours to find my way out to the main road in the dark. I finally located my jeep and started for Bogota. I stopped in the nearest village and managed to wake up a store owner long enough to use his telephone. I called Mr. Bascom and asked him to get the chief of police out of bed."

He looked disgusted as he continued, "The chief of police wasn't very happy about being yanked out of bed in the middle of the night. It was dawn by the time I got to Bogota, and the men I'd asked for still hadn't shown up."

He motioned to the soldiers, who now stood at ease, looking friendly and pleased. "I finally managed to get together a troop from the Colombian army and started back here, but when I reached the campsite and saw . . ."

He looked grim for a moment, then cleared his throat. "Well, for a moment, I didn't think I'd need any of them. Then I saw the tracks leading into the woods and realized that the guerrillas, at least, had escaped. I sent most of my men after them, hoping they'd taken you with them.

"I sent this party to check downstream. Then I saw fresh footprints running down this way along the cliff top—two sets of them fairly small."

He grinned at the two girls. "I figured that at least you two must be alive, so I headed down this way as fast as I could. And of course, you know the rest." After a pause, he added, "Okay, now tell me *your* story."

The three children let Uncle Pete explain what had happened since Steve escaped. Steve looked with respect at Estrella as Uncle Pete told of how she had rescued them. When Uncle Pete finished, Steve stood up.

"Well, now that we have you all safe and sound, let's get back to town. I imagine you could all use a good meal and some warm clothes, and some of you could sure use a bath!" He smiled at Justin and Uncle Pete.

Estrella and Jenny politely turned away as Justin stood up and awkwardly pulled on his mud-encrusted jeans and tennis shoes. He was stiff and sore all over and very thirsty, but the scenery no longer whirled around him when he moved. The mud that still caked his hair and face crackled with every movement, and large pieces of dry mud flaked off his jeans.

As the two girls turned around, Jenny giggled. Justin scowled at her. "What's so funny?"

Jenny's gold-brown eyes danced. "You should see yourself, Justin!" She broke into giggles. "You look like . . . like the Abominable Mudman!"

The sudden relief from the tension of the last two days was too much. Estrella started giggling, too, and Jenny was now holding her sides with helpless laughter. Uncle Pete's hearty "Ha, ha!" rang out from behind Justin, and even Steve and the soldiers were grinning broadly.

Justin looked down at the heavy, gray crust that covered even where Uncle Pete had tried to wipe him dry. He *did* look funny, he thought. The girl's giggles were contagious, and the dried mud crinkled around his mouth as he broke into a grin.

Steve interruped the relieved laughter. "If you can walk, Justin, let's get started. It's a long walk back to the road, even if we cut across from here."

Justin cautiously took a few steps, wincing as his bruised body protested. He was sore, but he could walk. As he followed Steve away from the bank, Justin turned for one last look.

There was no sign now of the bubbling stream, nor of the evergreen forest that had carpeted the mountain valley an hour ago. A tranquil, gray-brown lake now stretched from bank to bank. Only the drift of an occasional piece of debris, and the whistling pop of an enormous air bubble coming to the surface, showed that the *lahar* was still settling.

They took the hike back to the road very slowly. Once there, Steve left the three soldiers with the army transport truck, to wait for the rest of the soldiers. It was late afternoon before Justin joined the others in the lounge of the embassy guest house. A long, hot shower had washed away much of the stiffness, and with a very large meal under his belt, he felt much better.

The twins had just attempted another call to their parents when Steve walked in. To Justin's disappointment, there was still no answer at his home—not even the answering machine. His parents should be back from their camping trip by now!

Steve sat down and stretched out his legs. He too looked refreshed, his hair still wet from a recent shower. "That troop of soldiers just reported in. There's no sign of the guerrillas—they got completely away!"

"Good!" Estrella suddenly spoke up. Steve looked at her in surprise, and she said simply, "Well, they *were* kind to me. They were the only family I had."

Walking over to stare out the window, she added sadly, "Even if it *was* only because I could be of use to them."

"Well, I don't think it will make much difference," Uncle Pete put in. "With all our American families pulled out of the country and security tripled at the office, I don't think they'll bother Triton again."

He shook his head. "I'm afraid it may be a long time before we'll be sending married engineers and families back to Colombia. Perhaps one day there will be a true peace with the guerrillas."

"Well, it's all over for you three, anyway," Steve commented. "You are free to fly home anytime."

Jenny, curled up on the sofa beside Uncle Pete, looked over at Estrella, who still stood at the window. The long, shining curtain of hair hid her expression, but the slim shoulders drooped.

Jenny asked softly, "What about Estrella? What's going to happen to her?"

"Yeah, they can't put her in prison like those other guerrillas, can they?" Justin added anxiously. "She saved our lives!"

"No, of course they won't put her in prison," Steve assured them. "For one thing, she is only a child. And as you said, she is responsible for freeing the three of you."

"But where will she live?" Jenny asked. "Her 'family' is gone."

"I think I may have a solution to that," Uncle Pete said. "I've got a missionary friend here in Bogota . . ."

Justin grinned at his sister. He was beginning to think Uncle Pete had friends tucked away in every corner of the world.

"I called him," Uncle Pete continued, "and he thinks he may know of a home for her."

The sharp *ding-dong* of the front doorbell rang through the building. Uncle Pete stood up. "That may be him now."

He hurried out of the room, and Steve went with him to unlock the door. The twins walked over to join Estrella at the window. Like all windows they had seen in Colombia, this one was heavily barred. The window looked down onto the street that ran in front of the guest house. Through the slats of the venetian blinds, they could see a car pulled up at the front steps.

Estrella turned from the window, and the three children looked shyly at each other. So much had happened since the last time they had sat there that they didn't know what to say.

Justin broke the silence. "We haven't thanked you for saving our lives, Estrella. I was wrong about you. You really were our friend all the time. You could have been killed coming back for us like that."

"I had to do it," Estrella answered simply. "It was my fault that you were in danger."

Looking at Justin, she added, "You were right about Carlos. He never did really care about me. None of them did! They just thought I'd be useful to them."

Her head drooped. "At least they gave me schooling and

a place to sleep. I don't know what I will do now."

Justin and Jenny were saved from answering by their uncle's booming call. "Kids, come on down here! I've got some folks here for you to meet."

The twins started for the door. Estrella hung back until Jenny grabbed her by the hand and pulled her after them. "Come on, Estrella! He means you, too!"

Justin and Jenny hurried down the wide staircase, Estrella following reluctantly behind. Justin heard his uncle's deep voice above a chatter of voices in the receiving room. Pausing in the doorway, he saw his uncle talking among a lively group of people. There was a short, bearded man, whom Justin guessed was Uncle Pete's missionary friend, and a Colombian couple perhaps a few years older than the twins' parents.

Silence fell abruptly as the four adults caught sight of the children. Justin eyed the visitors as they rose to their feet. The Colombian man was tall and thin, with curly, dark hair and a kind face. His wife was slightly plump. Something in her expression reminded Justin of his mother, and he liked her at once.

Uncle Pete stepped forward. "Kids, this is my friend, George Elinger. He is a missionary here in Bogota. These are his friends—"

But he never got to finish his introduction. Justin suddenly realized that Estrella hadn't followed the twins into the room. She stood frozen in the doorway, her blue eyes wide and unbelieving as she stared at the Colombian couple.

"Doña Rosa?" Her voice was hardly above a whisper.

The Colombian lady turned toward the doorway with a jerk, astonishment on her plump face. Her dark eyes widened as she exclaimed, "Estrellita (Es-tray-yee-ta)!"

Estrella was moving now. Uncle Pete and Mr. Elinger looked at each other in bewilderment as she ran across the room and threw herself into the plump lady's arms. The tall, thin man moved close, an the room erupted into a babble of laughing and crying and Spanish chatter.

As Mr. Elinger moved away to join the excited group, Uncle Pete continued his introduction to the only two who were listening. "This is Mr. And Mrs. Gutierrez, friends of Mr. Elinger. They work with the street children here in Bogota. They have no children of their own, but have a house full of teenage girls they have adopted."

He eyed his grinning niece and nephew sharply. "Why do I get the impression you know more about our visitors than I do?"

Just then, Estrella pulled the plump, dark-haired lady across the room to where the three Parkers were standing.

"This is Doña Rosa," she said unnecessarily. "Don Eduardo is her husband . . . You remember them, the ones I told you about? They took me in and wanted me to be their own daughter. They didn't know it was me they had been asked to come here to visit. But they want me to be their daughter—even though I once ran away from them!"

She shook her head in amazement. "How ever did you find them? *I* didn't even know where they had gone!"

Justin shrugged, still hardly able to believe this new surprise himself. "We didn't! I guess God must have found them for you."

Doña Rosa obviously didn't understand a word of what was being said, but she was smiling broadly. Before Justin could move, she stepped forward and kissed him heartily on both cheeks. Then she kissed Jenny, bursting into a chatter of Spanish.

Estrella laughed at their astonished expressions. "She is thanking you for finding me—the Colombian way!"

It was a long time before all the chatter died away. But at last, Mr. Elinger and the Gutierrezes stepped out into the big entryway. Estrella hesitated as Doña Rosa waved a hand and called to her in Spanish.

Turning to the twins, she explained, "They want me to go with them tonight."

She added uncertainly, "I would like to see my new home, but I do not wish to leave you, my friends. Do you mind?"

"Of course not!" Justin assured.

Jenny added, "You go ahead, Estrella. You've probably got lots to talk about . . . We *will* see you again, won't we?"

"I will not let you go without saying good-bye," Estrella promised. After a quick hug, she was gone.

The guest house seemed strangely quiet with Estrella gone. "I sure wish Mom and Dad would answer the phone!" Justin told Jenny for the third time as he looked with little interest through an outdated *Popular Mechanics* magazine.

Neither paid any attention to the sound of footsteps in the hall outside the lounge. A moment later, Steve poked his head around the door and announced, "Some people here to see you, kids!"

The door swung open, and the twins jumped to their feet, the magazine falling unnoticed to the floor. "Mom! Dad!" they yelled together.

It was several minutes before Justin or Jenny even noticed Mr. Bascom standing patiently by the door. Mr. Parker was finally able to explain. "We got home from our camping trip last night and called the embassy here right away. We were . . . well, to put it mildly, we were upset when we heard you were missing. We caught the first flight to Bogota."

He paused, and Mrs. Parker went on. "Mr. Bascom had given us his number to call when we arrived. By the time we got here, he had heard from Steve that you were all safe. We called him from the airport, and he picked us up and brought us here."

A short time later, Justin and Jenny were squeezed in between their parents on the sofa. Mrs. Parker gasped in horror as they poured out the adventures of the last two weeks; Uncle Pete occasionally added a comment in his deep voice. Already, the fear, anger and hurt of the last hours were fading into exciting memories.

$$\sim\sim\quad\sim\sim\quad\sim\sim$$

It was very late before any of the Parkers got to sleep that night, but they were all up and at the airport early the next morning. Mr. Bascom had booked them on the first flight back to Seattle, with a brief stop at Miami. This time, Justin appreciated the feeling of security as he watched the soldiers make their rounds of the airport and search through every inch of their bags.

Estrella and her new parents arrived at the airport just in time to see them off. Her delicate features were alive with happiness as she told the twins, "I love my new home and Mama Rosa and Papa Eduardo. Remember that I told you they were moving to find a new job? It was then that they met this man, George Elinger. He was helping the *gamines*, the street children. Now they work with him."

She added with a smile, "There are four other girls living with us. They are very nice. Now I have sisters! But I will not forget that you two were my first true friends. You have taught me much. This time I will listen when Doña Rosa talks to me about God and forgiveness."

Turning to Justin, she said shyly, "Thank you for finding

out about my father. Steve told me that it was your idea. Now I can remember him with love."

"Justin! Jenny!" the twins' father called out, motioning impatiently. The loudspeaker had ordered the passengers to pass through the final checkpoint. Estrella threw her arms around Justin and Jenny and hugged them fiercely.

"I'll never forget you—*never!*" she said passionately. She turned without another word and was gone.

The final call came to board Flight 908 for Miami. Picking up his briefcase as the line of passengers began filing down the long, narrow corridor that connected the waiting area to the Avianca 747, Uncle Pete looked down at the twins.

"Well, kids, our trip is about over. I guess the rest of this summer is going to seem pretty quiet."

"I'm not so sure about that," Mr. Parker interrupted as he handed over their tickets. "I've got some plans of my own!"

He grinned down at his son and daughter. "Remember that I told you we'd finished that Boeing project earlier than I expected? Well, I think it's time for a real family vacation. I've had an invitation to visit a friend of mine on an Indian reservation in Montana. Are you interested?"

The sudden excitement on their faces was all the answer he needed. He turned to his brother as they filed onto the big plane.

"Speaking of that friend of mine, do you think you'd have time for a brief stop in Montana too? There are some strange things going on out there with that mineral prospecting operation I told you about . . ."

Justin's ears pricked up immediately. As he slung his handbag into the overhead rack and found a seat beside his father, he had a sudden feeling that his summer adventures weren't yet over.

Jenny was sandwiched between Uncle Pete and Mrs. Parker across the aisle. She was busily chattering to her mother as though she hadn't seen her in months. As the big jet lifted from the runway, Mr. Parker looked down at his son.

"You've gone through some frightening times in the last couple of weeks, Justin," he commented. His blue-green eyes that were so like Justin's twinkled as he continued. "I'll bet you kind of wish now that you'd settled for that dull summer vacation you were expecting."

"It *was* pretty scary sometimes," Justin admitted. "But I'm glad I came."

Justin's mind filled with memories.

He shook his head vigorously. "Yeah, I'm glad I came. I wouldn't have missed these last two weeks for anything!"

About the Author

Jeanette Windle grew up as a daughter of TEAM missionary parents. She has lived in six countries and is now in Bolivia, where her husband, Marty, serves as acting field director for Gospel Missionary Union. When in the States, they make their home in Seattle, Washington. She and Marty have four children.